EMMY KEEPS A PROMISE

EMMY KEEPS A PROMISE

Written and illustrated by
MADYE LEE CHASTAIN

New York
HARCOURT, BRACE AND COMPANY

LIBRARY OF CONGRESS CATALOG CARD NUMBER: 56-9200

PRINTED IN THE UNITED STATES OF AMERICA

For Maude Harmon Worcester

CONTENTS

1. EMMY'S PROMISE 3

2. A TASTE OF NEW YORK 20

3. NEW FRIENDS FOR EMMY 34

4. TEA PARTY 48

5. JENNY LIND 63

6. THE INVITATION 79

7. "AND THE PARTY IS TOMORROW" 93

8. CAPTAIN ANDY 102

9. THE DAUNTLESS 114

10. TROUBLE FOR CHRISTMAS 130

11. THE PRUITT PRIDE 149

12. EMMY KEEPS A PROMISE 164

EMMY KEEPS A PROMISE

·❦· 1 ·❦·

EMMY'S PROMISE

EMMY heard the clock strike four as she put the last of her clothes in her valise and closed it. She looked around the small room to see if she had forgotten anything. Outside, it was still midnight-dark without the faintest glimmer of the day to come.

There was a soft rap, and Aunt Hannah Pruitt opened the bedroom door. "Emmy, my child," she said in a low voice, "I want to speak to you a minute where Arabel can't hear." She came in and closed the door behind her. Aunt Hannah's eyes were a little red from the frequent tears she had been brushing aside all through breakfast.

"I declare, I hate to see you go off like this," she began. "I've said it before and I say it again. New York is no place for two girls to be going alone!" She dabbed at her eyes.

Emmy went over to her aunt and put her arms around her ample waist. "But you know why we're going, Auntie."

"It's all nonsense, a girl having a career!" said Aunt Hannah, tearful but cross. "Marriage is the proper career for a girl like Arabel. Now, if only she had accepted that nice boy, Clem Colver—and him right here next door practically and someday he'll own that farm you'll see—" Aunt Hannah began to cry again.

"But Arabel doesn't love Clem, Auntie," Emmy explained patiently. "And besides, she's determined to pay back the money you and Uncle Ben spent for her education. And this teaching job in New York is a wonderful opportunity for her."

"We never expected her to pay us back." Aunt Hannah wept softly into her handkerchief. She blew her nose and looked up. "It's that Pruitt pride. Stiff-necked pride I've always called it. A Pruitt never accepts anything he can't pay back!" She shook her head. "I know. I'm married to one. I can tell you now, if your Uncle Ben hadn't always been so proud and afraid he'd accept a favor from somebody, we wouldn't be as poor as we are today."

Emmy patted her aunt on the shoulder and tucked a loose strand of white hair back into her bun. "You mustn't worry," said Emmy.

Aunt Hannah wiped her eyes once more and straightened up. "Emmy," she said quickly, hearing Arabel's voice outside speaking to her uncle. "Promise me something! When you get to New York, if you meet a nice respectable young man, will you see to it that Arabel marries him? Then she can give up this silly idea of a career and settle down and be like all the other girls."

Emmy couldn't help smiling. "What could I do?" she said.

"You could do a lot! You're all Thatcher, Emmy, with your father's good horse sense and plenty of spunk! Now

4

Arabel is just like your mother was—*pretty* and *proud.*
Arabel's all Pruitt, I tell you." Aunt Hannah drew Emmy
close to her and said in a low tone but with emphasis, "Now
you listen to me, Emmy. I'm going to depend on you to
take care of Arabel. You've got gumption. I've seen that
all along. And you look out for a likely young man, too,
and see if you can't change her ideas about this career talk.
Marriage, that's the career for Arabel!"

"We'd better be starting if we're going to catch that
four forty-five for New York!" called Uncle Ben.

"I'm ready!" said Emmy.

"Mind you don't forget!" whispered Aunt Hannah.
"And write me how it comes along!"

Emmy promised she would, and they went out together
to join Arabel and Uncle Ben in the hall.

Twenty minutes later, they had reached the station and
were standing on the platform which was dimly illuminated
by two solitary lanterns. Around them the deep silence
that precedes the dawn was broken only by the sound of
the horses breathing and an occasional creak of harness
leather.

Emmy took a deep breath, and a little tremor went
through her. This morning was like a dream! She couldn't
remember ever having been anywhere else but Geneva,
and now she was on the brink of an entirely different life.
Before this day was over, they would be in New York,
where Arabel had so longed to go! What was it going to
be like? Emmy couldn't even imagine, but the excitement
of it all made her shiver again.

"You're cold!" scolded Aunt Hannah, reaching to tie Emmy's wool scarf more securely. "These chilly September mornings are treacherous. Now you just mind when you get to New York that you keep warmly dressed." She turned to Arabel, her voice breaking a little, "I declare, Arabel, I do feel nervous about you two children going off to New York on your own like this. No, I can't help it, I do!" And she found her handkerchief again and began to wipe her eyes.

Arabel gave an affectionate little laugh and hugged her aunt. "Now, now! We aren't going to go through all that again, are we, Auntie? You just mustn't worry about us like this. Besides, you forget I am nineteen years old and Emmy is already past eleven."

Emmy gave her sister a grateful glance. The way Arabel had said it made "past eleven" sound quite grown up.

"You wouldn't want me to miss this wonderful opportunity to teach in New York!" continued Arabel. "I think I am the luckiest person in the world to have known Miss Euphrasia Fenwick here in Geneva. And imagine her kindness in recommending me to her sister who has a school in New York!"

"You could have stayed here in Geneva," quavered Aunt Hannah.

"With only a part-time teaching position at Mrs. Hudley's, and no future at all?"

"You could have married Clem Colver," said her aunt.

"Oh, *Auntie!*" Arabel shook her head impatiently. "I won't think of marriage for *ever* so long!"

6

"But I promised your folks I'd always look after you. Me and your Uncle Ben." Aunt Hannah dabbed her eyes again.

"And you *have*, Auntie, you always have! You've both been wonderful to Emmy and me!" Arabel hugged her aunt again and said very cheerfully, "Now, you aren't to worry about us at all! Miss Fenwick's School for Young Ladies is very well known in New York, and you can write to us there until we get settled. Then I'll send you our address. We are going to be just fine! You'll see!"

Uncle Ben was taking his big gold watch out again. He had looked at it every two minutes since they had arrived at the station. "It's going to be just like that pesky train to be late!" he said gruffly. He swiped the back of his hand across his eyes and peered at the dial. "I'm bound if I can even see my watch in this sorry light."

Suddenly, the horses pricked up their ears, and Uncle Ben held up his hand for silence. Far away in the distance they could hear the puff-puff of the train's engine.

At the sound, Aunt Hannah broke into fresh weeping, and Arabel and Emmy both threw their arms around her again. "Aunt Hannah, *don't* cry!" said Emmy, tears beginning to roll down her own cheeks.

"Surely it would be better if Emmy stayed with us 'til she's a mite older!" wailed their aunt.

"Now, now, Hannah," Uncle Ben put in. "You know they've never been separated. It's only natural Arabel should want Emmy to go with her. After all, she'll be going to school at Miss Fenwick's. That was part of the

7

bargain. And Arabel's going to look after Emmy just like we would."

"And I'm going to look after Arabel!" said Emmy stoutly with a special nod to her aunt.

The train was in sight now, and in another moment it had clanged and swooshed to a stop, great clouds of steam billowing into the frosty morning air. There were last minute good-bys, and then Arabel Drusilla Thatcher and Emmaline Eliza Thatcher were on their way to New York.

"I'm so excited I can hardly breathe!" whispered Emmy as they settled their valises and bandboxes. "Is it really true we're going to New York? Pinch me!"

"Yes, we're going to New York," said Arabel, but in such a small voice that Emmy turned to look at her sister. Arabel's delicate, pretty face looked pale and her large dark eyes troubled. "What's the matter, Arabel?" Suddenly, Emmy was worried.

"I—I—I guess I'm a little scared," admitted Arabel and twisted her fingers together.

"But, Arabel, you seemed so *sure* all along!"

"I know, I know. But we are going so far from Geneva —and after all, I'm just a country school teacher—and New York is such a big, fashionable place—and—"

"Arabel Thatcher!" said her sister sternly. "You stop that! You're just as smart as anybody else and you're a wonderful teacher and you were the first student in all your classes at Sardley's Academy and you're perfectly well prepared to teach or Miss Fenwick wouldn't have engaged you and besides you've always got me!" she finished all in one breath.

"Yes," said Arabel, throwing her arms about Emmy. "I've always got you! And I don't know how I'd get along without you! I just *had* to bring you with me!"

"I should think so!" retorted Emmy. "I wouldn't have let you come without me! No indeed!"

It was the middle of the afternoon when they reached New York. They stood on the train platform while the people swirled about them. They kept close together with their valises and bandboxes held close and tried to keep from being pushed and bumped. All around them, people were being greeted, embraced, and carried off by friends and relatives. Everyone was laughing and talking at once, creating such a hubbub that the two girls felt confused.

"I was sure Miss Fenwick would meet us," said Arabel. She looked up and down the platform with a lost expression.

Emmy felt lost, too, but she couldn't let Arabel see it. "She's probably just late, that's all. Did she say definitely that she would meet us?"

Arabel raised a hand to her cheek with a distracted little gesture. "Oh, Emmy, I just can't remember now. I *thought* she said she would meet us!"

They looked up and down the platform once more. The last of the passengers were straggling off, repair crews were walking back and forth with oil cans looking at the wheels and undercarriages of the train, two porters were pushing loaded baggage trucks.

"There's no one else," said Arabel.

Emmy reached down and picked up half of the valises and bandboxes. "There's *no* reason to worry. We have Miss Fenwick's address and we'll just *go* there!"

"But can we find it?" Arabel was looking more worried all the time.

"Of course we can find it. We can—we can hire a hackney coach." Emmy gasped a little at her own remark. She had never been in a hired carriage in her entire life. But she had heard about them.

"Oh, I don't know—" said her sister.

When they reached the street, sure enough, there were a line of hackney coaches for hire.

"Wait!" said Arabel as Emmy moved forward toward one of them. "Don't get in until we ask how much the fare will be!"

Arabel approached the carriage and spoke to the burly man perched on the driver's seat. She came back to Emmy with a shocked expression. "I never heard of anything so outrageous!" she whispered. "He wants to charge seventy-five cents! Why, we could have several days' meals for that sum!"

"What will we do?" said Emmy. "Take one of those—those—" She pointed to the oversized stagecoaches lumbering down the street, one after the other.

"They're omnibuses," said Arabel. "But there are so many, and we don't know which one to take!"

The street was alive with bustle and noise. Crowds swarmed around them—bigger ones than Emmy had ever seen. "Well," she said practically. "We can walk. Let's ask someone where Miss Fenwick's is."

They waited until a kindly looking woman came along, and then they asked her for directions.

"Well, now," said the woman, eying their luggage. "It's a right smart piece to walk. Sure you hadn't better take a carriage?"

"Oh, no," said Arabel hastily. "We don't want one."

"We like to walk," said Emmy. "We can see more that way."

"I see. Well, then, you walk in this direction for about eleven blocks, more or less. That will bring you to Lafayette Place. The address you want is two blocks east on Eighth Street. You can't miss it."

"Two blocks east on Eighth Street," mumbled Emmy, determined to keep it straight in her mind. She dropped the woman a curtsy. "Thank you very much."

The woman smiled. "You're welcome, I'm sure. Enjoy your stay here." And as she walked off, they heard her say aloud to herself, "How nice to see fresh country girls. So mannerly."

"There! *Everybody* can see we're from the country!" said Arabel, turning very red in the face.

Emmy picked up her share of the luggage again. "I don't see anything wrong with being from the country and that nice woman didn't either. Come on, let's start to Miss Fenwick's."

The traffic was so heavy and the noise and crowds so bewildering that they stood on the corner for some time before they dared venture across. They waited until there was a fair-sized group making its way to the other side of the street, and then they followed.

"I've just never seen anything like this!" gasped Arabel. "How will we ever find our way about?"

"It isn't much like Geneva," grinned Emmy. "But isn't it exciting?"

Arabel nudged her a moment later. "See that elegantly dressed lady!"

A handsome woman swept by in voluminous, rustling skirts, immaculate in long white kid gloves and wearing a velvet bonnet covered with rosebuds, black lace, and satin ribbons. She gave off a delightful fragrance of white roses as she passed.

Emmy sniffed the air. "She certainly smells nice."

It was a long walk indeed to Miss Fenwick's. They stopped to rest every half block, but finally they reached Eighth Street and turned east.

"I don't think my arms will ever be the same," said

13

Emmy. She put down her luggage and stood flexing her arms as Arabel tugged at the bellpull on Miss Fenwick's door. They could hear the bell ring inside with a muffled faraway sound.

Arabel held her right arm across her waist very tightly. Emmy knew it was because Arabel had that empty scared feeling inside, but she pretended not to notice.

"Oh," said Miss Fenwick. "It's Miss Thatcher, I believe? I've been expecting you. This way." She briskly led the way down the hall to her office.

"We thought you were going to—" Emmy began, but Arabel nudged her hastily and shook her head.

Miss Fenwick was a small, thin woman with sharp black eyes. Her dark hair, parted in the middle, was drawn down over each cheek, and the rest was done in a tight, uncomfortable-looking bun. Arabel's hair, in contrast, was soft and fluffy. Although drawn back severely, it still escaped in soft ringlets and fell in a mass of curls where she had it pinned in the back. How pretty she is, thought Emmy. Soft black hair, great dark eyes, and cheeks still rosy from the country air.

Miss Fenwick was observing Arabel closely, too. "You are nineteen, Miss Thatcher?" she questioned. "I understand that you taught last year in Mrs. Hudley's School in Geneva?"

"Mrs. Hudley said she would write you," said Arabel.

"And so she did," admitted Miss Fenwick. "It's just that I pictured you rather differently." Although, in which way Arabel was different, she didn't go on to say.

14

Miss Fenwick turned to Emmy for the first time. "You are Emmaline?"

"Yes, Miss Fenwick," said Emmy and dropped her a second curtsy, not knowing what else to do.

"You know, of course, that we are very strict here in my school. I don't know what you have been used to in Geneva, but you will of course conform to all our rules and regulations here."

Emmy didn't reply but looked straight into Miss Fenwick's eyes.

"School begins promptly at nine o'clock. All pupils are required to be in their respective classrooms with their Bibles in hand. We always begin with prayer."

Emmy nodded.

"Pupils must be exceedingly quiet, with no conversation, laughter, or writing of notes. I will allow no loud talking, romping, or general noisiness in recess and under no circumstances will tolerate tardiness." She regarded Emmy closely. "Want of amiability merits a forfeit mark."

Emmy, who wasn't feeling very amiable at the moment, opened her mouth to reply, but Arabel hastily interrupted her to say, "I'm sure you'll find Emmy very amiable, Miss Fenwick!"

Miss Fenwick gave Emmy another long look and then turned back to Arabel. "You will have to hurry if you expect to find lodgings before nightfall. I was unable to do more than mark a few likely advertisements in today's *Tribune*. I have marked those where the addresses were reasonably close. I suggest that you go immediately and

15

see them. You may leave your luggage here and come back for it when you have engaged rooms."

"Whew!" said Emmy when they were on the street again, hurrying back toward Lafayette Place. "I don't think I'm going to like that old Miss Fenwick!"

"Don't say that, Emmy! We *must* like her! So much depends on it."

"I'll try to be good, Arabel. But I don't have to like her!"

"No," agreed her sister. "But it helps. Now, which of these shall we look at first? Here is an advertisement that says: *Pleasant furnished rooms to let with breakfast and tea. 11 Wooster Street.* Let's try that one. Miss Fenwick said Wooster Street was down this way."

The rooms were pleasant indeed, very large and well furnished, but the rent was so dear Arabel and Emmy thanked the woman and got out as quickly as possible.

"Let's go see this one on Spring Street. Come along, Emmy, it will be dark soon enough!" Emmy had been walking along looking at everything in this strange new city, especially the rows and rows of houses that looked so much alike and were built right on the street with no front yards as they had in Geneva. There were three little girls across the street rolling their hoops and laughing. Emmy wished she could say hello and make friends. Suddenly, the city looked very, very big and Emmy felt very, very small.

The rooms on Spring Street were down a dark hall and looked out on an even darker court. The bed had a large sunken place in the middle, and the spread wasn't clean. Arabel stood in the middle of the room and looked about her in a discouraged way.

The landlady stared at them. "You girls by yourselves? You got any baggage? I require all rent in advance, you know, and no late hours, mind."

Emmy didn't like *her* looks, either. Her hair was stringing down untidily, and her apron was even dirtier than the bedspread. Before Arabel could ask the rent, Emmy said in a determined voice, "Arabel, I don't think we could walk this far back and forth to Miss Fenwick's every day."

She quickly pushed Arabel ahead of her down the long dark hall and stairs. They were going out the front door before the landlady reached the bottom of the stairs, but they didn't miss hearing her parting words. "Well! And thank you so much my fine ladies! Thank you so much! Don't mind how much trouble you put people to—no, indeed—"

Emmy banged the front door shut, silencing the woman once and for all. They hurried down the street, relieved to get into the fresh air again. Then they began to giggle, for no reason at all.

"Honestly," said Arabel, wiping her eyes. "I don't know what we have to laugh about!"

"I don't either, but I feel better. Where do we go now?"

Arabel was looking at the paper again. "Here's one that sounds like it might be more reasonable. It says: *A furnished attic room, very clean, suitable for one or two*

ladies, is to let with breakfast and tea, 47 White Street.
An attic room ought to be cheaper."

Emmy agreed. "And it says *very clean*. That sounds
good. Where is White Street?"

They asked an elderly man standing on the corner, and
he directed them about six blocks farther downtown. "And
then turn right," he called after them as they started across
the street.

"People seem neighborly," said Emmy.

This sent Arabel into another fit of giggles. "I don't
think I ever heard New York called neighborly!"

At last they reached White Street and located number
forty-seven. Arabel reached for the bellpull, and it was
presently answered by a buxom, red-cheeked woman who
was wiping flour off her hands with a starched apron. A
starched *clean* apron, Emmy noted.

"You came about the room?" said the woman, smiling
at them. "Well, now you girls come right in. I'm Mrs.
Piddleby. Mrs. Ebenezer Piddleby. Ebenezer, that's my
husband."

Emmy couldn't hold back a smile, but Mrs. Piddleby
didn't notice. She was leading the way upstairs. "Right
this way, girls. It's up four flights, but I always say it's
good exercise, don't you?" Mrs. Piddleby was puffing
heavily by the time they reached the attic floor. "It's right
here. First door to the right." She opened the door and
shooed them in.

The room was sparsely furnished with a large double
bed, a washstand, a single chest of drawers, a small cane-

bottomed rocker, and a Franklin stove. Two dormer windows looked on the street, and the whole room was immaculately clean.

"How—how much is the rent?" asked Arabel.

It was so reasonable that both girls sighed with relief, and Arabel told Mrs. Piddleby they would get their valises directly and return as soon as they could. She opened her reticule and paid a week's rent in advance.

"That's fine," said Mrs. Piddleby, putting the money in her apron pocket. "And by the time you get back, I'll have your tea ready."

"Well there," said Emmy triumphantly when they were on the street again. "How's that for getting along in New York all by ourselves? We found Miss Fenwick's, and we've rented lodgings—with no help from anybody!"

Arabel wasn't as enthusiastic. "Do you realize we took lodgings Miss Fenwick hadn't marked? And they are a good fifteen blocks from the school? We'll have to walk it twice a day. And now we have to carry all our valises and bandboxes back down here tonight."

Even Emmy was wilted at the thought. After all, they had been up since three o'clock that morning, and she was beginning to feel as tired as Arabel looked. "Well," she said in her practical way, "the sooner we get started, the sooner we'll get back and have our tea and go to bed."

Arabel nodded in agreement, and they went off arm-in-arm toward the bustle and noise of Broadway.

2

A TASTE OF NEW YORK

I**T WAS** almost dark when Arabel and Emmy reached White Street with their valises and boxes. Wearily, they stopped to rest one last time before turning down the block. "I guess I was never so tired in my whole life!" said Emmy.

"I know." Arabel put an arm around her. "Just lean against me a minute and rest."

But Emmy shook her head. "If I do that, I'll go to sleep right here on the street."

"We could have taken an omnibus, as Miss Fenwick told us to, but we just *must* save every penny we have until we see how things are going to work out. I have only the little money I could save from my teaching last year and the money Uncle Ben made me take. And Emmy, I *must* pay all of that back!"

Emmy got to her feet and gave her sister a big, encouraging smile. "Of course we have to be careful! And we'll be as good as new tomorrow, and Miss Fenwick will never know the difference."

Mrs. Piddleby opened the door for them again. "Ah, there you are, girls! Take your things upstairs and then come right down to tea. I've just poured the hot water in the teapot."

The kitchen and dining room were on the floor below the parlor, half-below the ground and half-above so that the windows looked out on the sidewalk level. Seated a few minutes later at the big round table in the dining room, Emmy was fascinated to see a steady stream of feet going by the windows.

Mrs. Piddleby's family was gathered at the table, too.

"This is my husband, and my three girls, Dorcas, Verbena, and Mehitable."

Mr. Piddleby had bushy hair, bushy eyebrows, bushy mustaches, and—although Emmy didn't quite know how he achieved it—his clothes looked bushy, too. He bobbed his head to the girls in a friendly, embarrassed gesture.

"And this is my son, Nat," concluded his wife.

Emmy had wondered if Mrs. Piddleby might not have a nice, big, grown-up son with possibilities—for Arabel. She could hardly suppress a smile when she saw Nat was about ten years old, plump and rosy like his mother. The way he grinned and bobbed his head, though, was exactly like his father. The three little girls, all under six, were too shy to do anything but giggle.

"What a nice family you have, Mrs. Piddleby," said Arabel politely.

Mrs. Piddleby beamed. "I'm real pleased to have two nice girls like you come to live with us. You got any folks here?" She began to pour the tea.

Arabel explained why they were in New York.

"Well, now, what do you think of that, Ebenezer? Takes pluck to come here all alone like that, don't it?" Mrs. Piddleby fetched a large covered dish from the sideboard and took the lid off. "Steamed clams," she announced. "Here's the melted butter."

So *that* was the smell they had noticed as they came into the house! They had smelled it all the way up to their attic room. Emmy looked at the bowl of clams doubtfully. She had never eaten clams, and she wasn't at all sure she liked the way they looked. Arabel nudged her foot under the table.

"Nice, an't they? No fresher clams in New York than we got. No indeedy. That's because Mr. Piddleby's in the clam business. Yes, he is."

Mr. Piddleby grinned and bobbed his head again, looking very pleased.

All the children began to reach into the dish, taking out handfuls of clams, making a loud clatter as they did so.

"Now, now!" scolded Mrs. Piddleby. "Leave some for the young ladies! Nat! Mind your manners! Don't take too many at once! My lands, that boy!"

Arabel took several clams and put some on Emmy's plate, since Emmy had made no move to take any herself.

There was a cheerful hubbub at the table as Mrs. Piddleby and Arabel carried on the conversation, Mr. Piddleby and Nat dipped and slurped their clams, and the three little girls giggled.

Emmy gingerly pulled a clam out of its shell with her fork and dipped it into the melted butter. She hesitated a minute, closed her eyes, and popped the clam into her mouth. She chewed thoughtfully. Well, it wasn't so bad she guessed, since she was very hungry, but she was sure clams would never be one of her favorite dishes.

When the clam bowl was empty, Mrs. Piddleby went to the kitchen and filled it again. "Very nourishing, clams," she told them.

Emmy ate three more, and decided she had had enough. Besides, by the time she had finished two slices of bread and butter with plum jam for dessert, she had begun to feel so sleepy that she actually caught herself nodding twice.

"Well, now," said Mrs. Piddleby. "I guess you girls are pretty tired after this long day. I think you'd better get right up to bed before somebody has to carry one of you."

Emmy roused at that and smiled apologetically. Then, she and Arabel climbed the long flights to their room. They were too tired to do more than get into their nightdresses and fall into bed.

"We'll straighten up tomorrow," said Arabel drowsily.

But Emmy didn't answer. She was already fast asleep.

Church bells and peddler's cries awoke them in the morning. Close by, a deep-voiced bell clanged slowly. Farther away, two higher-pitched and more silvery-toned bells played an accompaniment. Emmy sat up in bed and listened delightedly.

"Hot muf-fins!
Hot muf-fins!
Get your hot muf-fins!"

23

called a voice under their windows. Someone else was crying vegetables. It was a woman's voice.

> "New potatoes!
> Red, ripe tomatoes!
> Pota-toes! Toma-toes!"

Another voice joined the clamor in the street.

> "My clams I want to sell today!
> The best of clams from Rockaway.
> And if you don't believe it's true,
> Come buy my clams and then you'll know.
>
> Come ye that have money and I that have none!
> Come buy my clams and let me go home!"

Downstairs a window banged open, and Mrs. Piddleby's voice rang out. "You can go home *now*, Samuel Snacker! Get away from here with your week-old clams! You know my Ebenezer's clams are the best clams in New York! Get off our block! Get off our block, I say!"

"I got a right to sell my clams wherever I want!" the clam man argued back.

"Them clams you got an't fit for pigs!" yelled Mrs. Piddleby. "They're popped open before you sell 'em! That's a fact!"

"Not true! Not true!" screamed the man.

"My heavens!" Arabel got out of bed and ran to the window.

Emmy was beside her in a moment, and together they leaned out to watch. They could see the red-faced clam man shaking his fist at Mrs. Piddleby. But he couldn't get the better of the argument. Mrs. Piddleby was threatening to get a dishpanful of hot water, and when she left the window to fetch it, the man beat a hasty retreat in the direction of Broadway.

Emmy chuckled. "It certainly isn't *quiet* here like it was in Geneva!"

They were dressed and had just finished making their bed when one of Mrs. Piddleby's little girls knocked on the door. She stood looking at Emmy and giggling, one foot twisted around the other. Emmy had to coax her to speak.

"Let's see now, which one are you? Mehitable?"

The little girl shook her head and went into a fit of giggles.

"Dorcas?"

This brought forth more head-shaking and giggling.

Emmy was beginning to laugh, too. "Well, then you *must* be Verbena."

The little girl doubled over with laughter.

Emmy leaned against the door and laughed, too. She shook her head at Arabel to show she didn't know *why* she was laughing.

"It's catching," said Arabel, chuckling a little herself.

"They call me Beenie," said the little girl, at last.

"Oh, I see, Beenie. Well, did you come to tell us something?"

This sent Beenie off into another spasm of tittering, and

Emmy was about to give up when the little girl finally managed to gasp out, "Mama says breakfast is ready."

"I never thought she'd make it," said Arabel as they went down the stairs.

The Piddleby family was seated at the round table again.

"Good morning," Arabel and Emmy greeted them.

"Good morning, girls. And a good morning it is, too. Look at that sunshine!" beamed Mrs. Piddleby, looking in fine humor after her triumph over the clam man.

Mr. Piddleby and Nat grinned and bobbed their heads. The three little girls giggled in unison.

"While I'm pouring your tea, you help yourself to the clams," said Mrs. Piddleby heartily. "There's fried clams in this dish and clam fritters in this one. Nice fresh muffins right here in this dish towel to keep 'em hot."

Emmy winced and threw Arabel a quick look. Clams for breakfast!

Arabel nudged Emmy's foot again. "Will you have fried or fritters, Emmy?"

"Fritters," replied Emmy reluctantly. The fritters didn't look so much like clams.

"Some folks like porridge or smoked herring or eggs and fat bacon or even pancakes, but *I* say there's nothing so nourishing as a good mess of clams to start the day off!" Mrs. Piddleby took a generous helping of both kinds of clams on her own plate.

Emmy's mouth watered at the very mention of pancakes, but she determinedly put her fork into a clam fritter and lifted it to her mouth. She managed to get one down and then finished her breakfast with muffins. There was no jam on the table this morning, and the butter tasted a little rancid—not fresh and sweet like their country butter in Geneva.

After breakfast, Emmy and Arabel spent a half hour emptying their valises into neat piles in the chest of drawers in their room.

"There." Arabel surveyed their work with satisfaction. "All your things are in the second and fourth drawers, and my things are in the first and third drawers. Now, the rest of our clothes in the bandboxes will just have to stay where they are, and I think they'll go under the bed nicely. Yes, they will," she said, sliding one under.

Emmy had been a little impatient. "Everything looks neat now, doesn't it, Arabel? Quick, let's put on our bonnets and go for a walk! We haven't seen anything of the city yet!"

"Yes, let's," said Arabel. "But we must be very careful to watch the time. Miss Fenwick said I was to be at the school promptly at one o'clock."

"But school doesn't start until Monday!" protested Emmy, who thought it would begin soon enough as it was.

"She wants to explain the routine at the school. If she doesn't, I won't know what to do next Monday. I'm sure everything will be different from Mrs. Hudley's in Geneva. After all, that's just a country school, and this is New York."

"Now, Arabel!" Emmy scolded. "You're not to talk like that! Anyone would think you hadn't won the highest honor at Sardley's Academy—the *Jeffronia Arilda Packington* prize!"

Arabel grinned at her young sister. "I'm sure no one in New York ever heard of Jeffronia Arilda Packington."

"You won it, anyway," persisted Emmy. "And you're going to be a big success at Miss Fenwick's."

"Emmy," said Arabel. "You've got twice as much spunk as I have. Aunt Hannah always did say you were just like Father. And you know the stories about him and how courageous *he* was."

"Maybe," said Emmy. "But Mother was the *prettiest*, Aunt Hannah always said. And you're like Mother. Uncle Ben said so, too."

"Pretty!" scoffed Arabel. "What I need right now are brains!"

"You've got those, too," said her sister loyally. "What's that noise? And all that ringing?"

A clamor of shouting and bell-clanging drew nearer as they came to the corner of Broadway and Bleecker Street. With a screeching of iron tires on the cobblestoned street, a fire engine careened around the corner, scraping the curbstone. Firemen in red-flannel shirts, black trousers, boots, and high leather hats were holding onto each side of the long pole attached to the front of the fire engine. This way they pulled it very fast while the runners kept in advance of the engine and shouted everyone out of the way. Passers-by turned and began to run in the direction of the fire, too, which, Emmy could see, was west of Broadway about two blocks away. Dark smoke was boiling up over the rooftops.

"Let's go, too, Arabel!"

"I should say not!" said Arabel, firmly holding her sister's arm.

Suddenly, a small figure shot around the corner of Bleecker Street and was going too fast to stop when he saw Emmy.

"Oof!" said Emmy, knocked off her feet and sitting down hard on the pavement. It had almost knocked the breath out of her.

The little boy had sat down hard, too, and scraped his knee besides. He was rubbing it now. In a moment, he scrambled up and went tearing off again after the fire engine without so much as a word of apology or a by-your-leave.

"Well!" Emmy picked herself up and brushed her skirt, side-stepping just in time to avoid two more people dashing off to the fire.

Arabel laughed. "As you said this morning, it isn't as quiet as Geneva!"

They continued along Broadway, fascinated with the sights and sounds and smells. Shop after shop after shop lined the long thoroughfare as far as they could see. "I guess it's like this all the way to the bay!" said Emmy.

The sidewalks were thronged with people, and the noise of the heavy traffic was deafening. Horse-drawn omnibuses, wagons, and fashionable carriages with matched bays, sorrels or strawberry roans struggled for right of way in the dense traffic. It seemed to Emmy that vehicles were going in all directions at random, and she couldn't imagine how they would ever get untangled.

"The shops!" said Arabel. "Look at this pastry store!"

They peered in the bakery window at the cakes displayed. Some of them were six tiers high and elaborately decorated with icing, candy roses, and cupids.

"The one with the pink candy cupids is mine," announced Emmy. "And you may have the six-tiered one with the white icing and the roses. It looks like a wedding cake."

"Now what would I be doing with a wedding cake?" said Arabel, turning a little pink.

"You'll need it sometime," said Emmy.

"Not any time soon!" was Arabel's crisp reply.

Emmy stole a glance sideways at her sister who was beginning to have that determined look around her mouth again. Emmy sighed. Aunt Hannah was right. Arabel was all Pruitt, and changing her mind about anything was going to be quite a lot to manage.

Arabel had moved on to the next store window. "Buttons!" she gasped. "Millions of them!"

It did look as if someone had put them in the window by the shovelful. "They must be two feet deep," mused Emmy. She bent down and pointed to one small red button right on the very bottom, pressed next to the window glass. "I wonder what would happen if I went into the store and asked for this one little button right down here?"

Arabel laughingly pulled her on to the neighboring shop which sold ribbons.

"I love a pretty ribbon," sighed Arabel. "Just look at that elegant rose and blue satin one with the gold thread —*oh!*"

"What is it?" said Emmy, peering at the ribbon and then the price card under it. Then she said "*Oh!*" too.

The card read: *Finest imported French Ribbon worthy of a Queen. $200.00 per yard.*

"Two hundred dollars for a yard of ribbon?" Arabel was horrified. "Why, that's—that's—downright sinful!"

Emmy had been inspecting the rest of the display. "Here's a piece that says *two cents per yard*, so maybe that makes it all right."

"Well! I must say they have quite a price range!"

"I'm hungry!" announced Emmy.

"So am I. Let's see what we can find. Of course we don't dare go to a restaurant; it would be too dear."

"Let's buy something in a shop and then go somewhere and eat it," suggested Emmy.

They noticed there were also shops down the side streets, and they decided it might be better to try one of them. They passed a greengrocer's and a bootmaker's. Farther down the block a little shop window displayed baked rolls and pastries and a few dishes of cooked foods. A delicious, mouth-watering aroma met them at the door.

They hesitated a minute and then went in. There were two other customers being waited on, which gave Arabel and Emmy time to look around.

One of the customers pointed to some semicircular pastries and said, "I'll have six *rissoles*. Are they chicken today?"

The dark-haired woman behind the counter replied, "Oui, monsieur. Today zey are chicken."

Emmy whispered to Arabel. "I thought they were apple turnovers maybe."

"They look good," said Arabel. "Let's see how much they are."

"Loaf of French bread and a half-pound of marinated lentils," said the second customer.

"*Everything* looks good," whispered Emmy again.

They ended by buying two *rissoles* apiece and two fat, glossy rolls the woman called *brioche*. They carried their lunch, wrapped in a square of paper, until they came to a small park, where they sat down on a bench and happily settled themselves to eat. "Did you know that was a French food store?" Arabel asked her sister. "Let's see what these *rissoles* are like."

"M-m-m," said Emmy appreciatively as she bit into one. It was a flaky pastry filled with a delicious mixture of minced chicken and spices. "What a wonderful change!"

"It *is* different from Aunt Hannah's cooking, isn't it?"

"I didn't mean that," said Emmy. "I meant it was a wonderful change from *clams!*"

•3•

NEW FRIENDS FOR EMMY

"I JUST wish I had Uncle Ben's gold watch!" panted Arabel, as she and Emmy half-trotted, half-ran up Broadway toward Lafayette Place and Miss Fenwick's. "Do you see a clock in any of these stores?"

"I saw one a block or so back. It said twenty-five minutes past eight."

"Oh-h-h!" wailed Arabel, breaking into a full run. "If we're late our very first morning, we might as well turn right around and go back to Geneva on the first train!"

"We can't run all the way!" gasped Emmy, trying to keep up.

"We certainly can!" Arabel caught hold of Emmy's arm to help her along faster.

By the time they arrived at Miss Fenwick's door, they were panting and disheveled. "Oh, how do I look?" whispered Arabel in a frantic voice. "I wanted to look so neat."

"Smooth your hair," advised Emmy. "It's blown a little."

Arabel hastily smoothed the curls down and pinned her back hair again.

Entering the hall, they made their way to the cloakroom,

where some of the pupils were already putting away their wraps.

"I'll hang up your cloak, Arabel. You run along," whispered Emmy.

"Oh, thank you! I'll see you later." Arabel, looking pale and nervous, hurried down the hall toward Miss Fenwick's office.

A chubby, red-haired girl was hanging up her cloak beside Emmy's. "Hello," she said in a whisper. "You are new, aren't you?"

Emmy nodded. "I'm Emmaline Eliza Thatcher. Call me Emmy."

"My name is Polly Tyler," said the girl, still whispering. "Where are you from?"

"Geneva," said Emmy, whispering, too.

"Oh!" said Polly. "Switzerland?"

Emmy shook her head. "New York."

Then they both giggled. Suddenly Polly clapped her hand over her mouth and shook her head at Emmy. "Sh-h-h!" she said.

"Why are we whispering?" asked Emmy who was beginning to be very puzzled by it all.

"Miss Fenwick," said Polly. "She doesn't allow any loud talking in the classrooms or halls."

"But do we have to whisper all the time? We wouldn't be talking *loud*."

"Miss Fenwick calls anything above a whisper *loud*."

Emmy sighed. There was no doubt about it; she was

35

not going to like that old Miss Fenwick! But she would try and mind all the rules for Arabel's sake.

Two more girls came in. "Hello, Polly," they said and looked at Emmy with interest.

"This is Emmy Thatcher," Polly introduced her. "These are my friends Dodie Mallow and Lissa Spenlow, and here comes Amanda Boddifer."

The girls gathered around Emmy, whispering. Dodie was pale, pale blonde—even her eyelashes were golden—while Lissa's hair was shiny brown and done up in tight fat curls. Her pretty blue eyes were smiling at Emmy. "Where are you from?"

"From Geneva. New York," she added so there would

be no mistake this time. "My sister Arabel is going to be the new teacher here."

"You mean Miss Fenwick isn't going to teach all the classes?" squealed the girls, forgetting themselves for a moment.

"How perfectly wonderful!" said Lissa Spenlow.

"*What* is all this commotion and loud talking?" demanded a voice behind them.

"Oh!" The girls jumped guiltily.

Miss Fenwick had an ominous frown on her face. "You will go into your classroom and sit down like ladies! *Quietly!*"

The girls tiptoed into their classroom and took their seats. At the end of one long bench there was a card that said *Emmaline.* Emmy went over to it and sat down. Presently, she noticed Lissa was trying to get her attention. Then Lissa held up her Bible.

Emmy jumped up and ran on tiptoe to the cloakroom and got her Bible. She just made it back to her seat when Miss Fenwick came in. Emmy smiled her thanks to Lissa who winked back.

After Bible reading and prayer, Miss Fenwick began the morning with a drill in spelling.

As each girl was called on in turn, she rose, curtsied, and spelled her word. Emmy watched closely so she would know just what to do. When Miss Fenwick came to her, she said, "Emmaline, spell contradictory."

Emmy gulped. It was a long word, and she was not sure she knew it, but she had to try. She rose from her seat, curtsied, and spelled the word by syllables, slowly and carefully.

Miss Fenwick nodded her head. "Correct," she said briskly, and Emmy sat down with a sigh of relief. At least she had made a good beginning.

After the spelling they had a lesson in grammar and a half hour's practice in penmanship.

The last morning class was music. Miss Fenwick went out to the class across the hall, and Arabel came in. Emmy looked at her quickly to see if she was still nervous. Arabel, however, was looking more composed, and some of the color had come back into her cheeks. Emmy was very proud of her as she stood before the class and spoke to the students.

"Please open your song books to page thirteen. Let us try 'Under the Greenwood Tree' in unison at first, and then I should like the first two rows to sing the first voice part and the second two rows to sing the second voice part in harmony." Arabel blew a note on her pitch pipe, and they began to sing.

The sound was dismal. "Oh, dear," murmured Arabel. "Perhaps I'd better sing it through once. Listen, carefully, to the tune." She began to sing in a sweet, clear, melodious voice.

Emmy watched the other girls begin to sit up and listen. Arabel's voice was enchanting, and Emmy was happy to see that the others thought so, too.

"Now, let's try it once more." Arabel blew on the pitch pipe again and beat the time with her hand.

When they had gone through the song several times, Arabel said, "That was very nice. Now let's turn to page fifteen and sing 'Robin Adair.' "

"You sing it first, Miss Thatcher," begged Lissa.

"Yes, do!" the others joined in.

"You must know how 'Robin Adair' goes," said Arabel in surprise.

"But you sing so *pretty*, Miss Thatcher!" said Dodie.

Arabel flushed a little, but Emmy could see she was pleased. "Well, if you'd like me to—" And she began to sing the old song so sweetly that all the girls sat hushed, listening.

She had almost reached the end of the song when Miss Fenwick strode in. "Miss Thatcher! I don't believe it is necessary for you to waste time giving an exhibition of your singing ability. This class knows 'Robin Adair' perfectly well. Kindly spend your classroom time in instructing the *pupils!*"

Arabel flushed a deep red, and her mouth trembled a little for just an instant. Then she said in a low voice, "I'm sorry, Miss Fenwick."

"But we *asked* her to sing it for us!" Lissa burst out.

"Melissa Spenlow, that will be one forfeit mark for you, for loudness and for speaking out of turn!"

Lissa's face turned almost as red as Arabel's, but Lissa's was flushed from anger, as anyone could see. She pushed out her lower lip and stared at Miss Fenwick with resentful eyes.

Miss Fenwick stared back at her sharply. "And there

will be a second forfeit mark for you, Melissa, for sullen-
ness." She turned on her heel and went out.

Polly Tyler turned around after Miss Fenwick's retreating figure and stuck out her tongue. Emmy could hardly
hold back a giggle; Polly had so well expressed what
everybody was feeling!

For the remainder of the music hour, all the girls made
a special effort to sing well and to keep in time, and Emmy
could tell they were doing it for Arabel's sake. When they
were dismissed for lunch, Lissa came over and whispered
in Emmy's ear, "I just *love* your sister! She is *so* sweet and
pretty. And that terrible Miss Fenwick was just plain
mean!'"

"I'm sorry you got the two forfeit marks," Emmy told
her.

"Pooh!" said Lissa. "I always get forfeit marks."

"You have such a beautiful voice, Miss Thatcher!"
Polly Tyler told Arabel. "Are you going to hear Jenny
Lind sing next Wednesday evening at Castle Garden?"

"No, but I've heard of her," said Arabel.

"She's called the Swedish Nightingale," declared
Amanda. "Papa has tickets for our family. This is the
first time Miss Lind has been in this country."

"Mr. Barnum of Barnum's Museum has brought her
over," said Dodie. "Oh, my, *everybody's* talking about
her! My mother bought me a pair of Jenny Lind gloves
and a Jenny Lind fan to carry," she finished importantly.

The girls got out their lunch baskets, and each very
carefully spread a large white napkin over her portion of

the long desk in front of her. On this was laid the food.

"Be careful of crumbs!" warned Lissa. "Miss Fenwick can see a crumb from across the room."

No wonder everyone is hovering over her napkin and eating so carefully, thought Emmy.

"Crumbs merit a disgrace mark." Dodie painstakingly brushed a crumb off a ruffle and dropped it onto her napkin.

Emmy sighed. In Geneva, the pupils had gathered together in the big schoolyard under the red maples and had eaten in peace, laughing and talking as much as they pleased.

Walking back to their lodgings with Arabel that afternoon, Emmy was thoughtful.

Presently, Arabel slipped her arm through her sister's. "You're very quiet," she said. "Homesick for Geneva?"

"No, not really," Emmy replied slowly. "But everything's very different, isn't it? And that old Miss Fenwick—"

"I know, Emmy, but this was just the first day. It will be better, you'll see."

"Sure," replied her sister. "I don't care about me, but I hated her talking to you like that!"

"Let's not think about it any more. Why, there's an advertisement for Jenny Lind's concert—the one the girls were talking about!"

Arabel was pointing to an omnibus going by with a huge sign plastered across it. *P. T. Barnum presents Jenny*

Lind, the Swedish Nightingale, first concert in this country! "I'd love to hear her."

"Well, why don't we go?" said Emmy.

"Oh, we couldn't! It would be too expensive."

They walked on in silence for a while, and then Arabel said, "I just have to find some other work."

"You're going to leave Miss Fenwick's?" gasped Emmy.

"No, no. I mean in addition to Miss Fenwick's. After all, school dismisses at two o'clock, and I have the rest of the afternoon to do something else. I think I'll buy a *Daily Tribune* and look at the advertisements."

"It costs two cents," Emmy cautioned her.

"It may prove worth it," said her sister.

They sauntered down Broadway, looking in all the shops again, bought their paper and turned the corner of White Street.

The minute they opened the front door, an unmistakable odor of clams assailed their noses.

Emmy groaned. "Not again!"

"She's bound to have something else eventually," whispered Arabel as they went up the stairs.

"Can't we go out for tea?"

"We're paying for our breakfast and tea here, Emmy. We just have to eat it. We can't pay for our meals twice."

"No, I guess not," said Emmy. "But we had *clam muffins* for breakfast this morning!"

Arabel giggled. "I didn't know you could put clams in muffins!"

"Mrs. Piddleby can put clams in anything," said Emmy dejectedly.

As they reached the attic floor, they heard tittering.

"That sounds like it's in our room!" said Arabel. She stepped up to the door softly and opened it with one quick gesture.

The three little Piddleby girls were standing in the middle of the room dressed in Arabel's and Emmy's clothes. They squealed in surprise at seeing the two older girls and promptly hid their faces like ostriches and went into a fit of giggles.

Dorcas was just barely visible in Arabel's best green merino, while Beenie was wearing Emmy's straw bonnet and her red-wool short cloak. The rest of their clothes were strewn around the room in the greatest confusion.

"Why, shame on you!" scolded Emmy. "Shame on you! See how you've mussed and wrinkled everything."

There was no answer from the three little girls except more giggling. They were still hiding their faces in their hands.

Emmy took her straw bonnet off Beenie's head and then got her out of the red cloak. This presented difficulties, since Beenie tried to keep her face hidden at the same time.

Arabel was struggling with Dorcas. "Now, you'll just have to get out of my dress! And you really mustn't do this again. It's naughty to go into other people's rooms and put on their clothes."

At last, they got their dresses off the children and shooed

them out of the room. They could hear them giggling all the way down the stairs.

"Just look at this!" Arabel motioned around the room. "And we had made things so orderly."

With a sigh, they set to work straightening and folding and putting away. Finally it was done, and Arabel sat down in the rocker to look at the advertisements in the *Tribune*. She read down the column for a moment, and then she sat up suddenly. "Listen to this, Emmy! *Wanted: Young person, schooled in voice and harmony, capable of instructing beginners, one or two hours a day. Select Music Academy. Professor Sollini, 280 Houston Street.* There! That sounds perfect! I'll go to see Professor Sollini immediately after school tomorrow!"

Emmy became thoughtful. *Professor Sollini.* It had a fascinating foreign sound. Perhaps *he* would be the one for Arabel! He was probably extremely tall and of course very handsome. Blue eyes? No, no. Most likely dark eyes —and wavy hair and perhaps side whiskers. Emmy frowned slightly. She wasn't sure she liked those side whiskers on him. Well, she could take them off. There, he looked much better without them. And he probably sang all day long in a beautiful tenor voice, and he and Arabel could sing duets together—

Emmy came out of her reverie with a start at the sound of Mrs. Piddleby's voice bawling up the stairs, "Tea is ready! Tea is ready!"

The two girls tidied themselves hurriedly and went downstairs to the kitchen level.

"Here we are!" said Mrs. Piddleby cheerfully. "Sit right down, girls. I've fixed something different for our tea."

"Thank goodness," murmured Emmy, perking up.

Mrs. Piddleby bustled into the kitchen and came back with the largest iron skillet Emmy had ever seen. She set it on a trivet in the middle of the table and took the cover off. "There!" she beamed. "A clam pancake! Did you ever see anything prettier? There's only a few people, if I do say so, who can make 'em."

Emmy looked at the huge flat pancake and then looked out the window. Feet were going by in a steady stream. There went a workman's heavy boots, caked with clay. Then children's feet skipping along, a gray cat, two full-flounced skirts followed by more boots—and none of them, *none* of them, going home to clams! Surely, there weren't any more clams left in New York after the Piddlebys had taken their share. Arabel was nudging her foot again.

"Stop woolgathering, Emmy. Mrs. Piddleby has cut you a slice of pancake."

"We always called it clamcake in our family," said Mrs. Piddleby chattily. "Papa always put catsup on his, but my brother Dordle always preferred molasses."

Molasses? Emmy wasn't quite sure the bite of clam cake she had just swallowed was going to stay swallowed.

"Drink your tea," advised Arabel quickly.

"Yes, indeedy," continued Mrs. Piddleby. "Clams are very nourishing. By next spring, you girls will be nice and plump. Fill out all those hollows with clams, that's what we'll do."

At Emmy's horrified expression, Arabel suddenly coughed into her napkin and didn't recover for a minute or so.

Well, thought Emmy desperately, I know what *I'm* going to do. I'm going to look for a job myself. And then we'll move right out of this house before Arabel and I both turn *into* clams!

4

TEA PARTY

IN SCHOOL, the next morning, Lissa hurried in just before class began and motioned excitedly to Emmy. "I have something to tell you!" she whispered across Polly and Amanda. Just then, however, Miss Fenwick came in, which put an end to all whispering.

Once, during writing class, Lissa tried to slip Emmy a note, but Miss Fenwick watched them all so sharply that Lissa finally gave up.

As soon as class was dismissed for lunch, Lissa scurried over and said excitedly, "Oh, Emmy, I told my Aunt Abbie and my grandfather all about you and your sister and how pretty she sings and that you're new in town, and they both want to meet you! Could you come to tea this afternoon at four o'clock?"

Emmy was delighted, and they both went in search of Arabel. She was in the other classroom across the hall with the younger children, who were eating their lunches, too.

"That will be lovely," said Arabel. "Thank your aunt and grandfather for us. It's very kind of them."

"And Mr. Bramble will be there, too. My Aunt Abbie

is engaged to him, and they're going to be married in November or December when my cousin Andy gets home. Oh, I wish Cousin Andy were home right now," sighed Lissa. "That would make it a *real* party!"

Lissa said this in such an affectionate tone that Emmy looked at her and smiled. "Who is your cousin Andy?"

"*Just* my favorite person in the whole world!" said Lissa. "He lives with us when he isn't on the *Dauntless*."

"What's the *Dauntless?*"

"Oh!" said Lissa dreamily. "She's the most beautiful clipper ship in Grandfather's line! She's so trim and so fast and so—" She paused for lack of a word expressive enough. "And Cousin Andy is her captain."

"He must be very old," said Emmy. The only sea captain she had ever known had been old Cap Bolton who had been a whaler for years before he retired to live with his daughter in Geneva. He was ancient and grizzled with iron gray hair and a perpetual squint as if he were looking out to sea.

"Yes," nodded Lissa. "He's *pretty* old. He's twenty-five. And he's the best and cleverest captain in the clipper trade! Nobody can make the run from New York to China and back as fast as Cousin Andy and the *Dauntless!*" She sighed, just thinking of it. "And he's so much fun!" continued Lissa, warming to her favorite subject. "I can't wait 'til he gets home! And he always brings me such wonderful presents!"

"He sounds awfully nice," said Emmy thoughtfully. "Is he married?"

"Oh, no," said Lissa. "But lots of girls have wanted to marry him. At least they acted like it. He's very handsome, you see, and—"

Emmy didn't hear the rest, for she was thinking very hard. Perhaps this was the one for Arabel! Well, anyway, there were now two prospects—Professor Sollini and Lissa's cousin Andy. She'd have to tell Aunt Hannah in her next letter.

When school was out, Arabel and Emmy hurried because on their way back to their lodgings they wanted to stop at the Select Music Academy and see Professor Sollini about the advertisement in the *Tribune*.

A complexity of sounds greeted them as they approached the front door of the music academy. Off-key scales were being played on a violin, someone was hammering away at a piano, and in the background several different voices could be heard, each singing a different tune.

Arabel made a little face as if her ears hurt.

The door opened, and a tall, sparse maid in a large white apron and a cap very much askew said, "Yes?" She was scowling.

Arabel looked taken aback. "Is—is Professor Sollini in?"

The maid snorted. "Oh, *him*. That way." And she motioned over her shoulder with her thumb toward a door on the left. "Can't you tell by the noise?" she said sourly and promptly left them there. In a moment she had disappeared down the hall towards the rear.

Arabel looked at Emmy helplessly. "I—I thought she would announce us."

"Go on," said Emmy. "I guess this is the way they always do it."

"No, no, no!" shouted a voice through the door on the left. "No, no, no! PLEASE! PLEASE! I say *please*, Miss Wells. NOT through the nose! You see? Now, once again, with the throat open, PLEASE!"

Emmy's mouth opened in surprise! Could this be the handsome Professor Sollini?

Arabel hesitated with her hand on the doorknob.

"Go on!" urged Emmy.

Arabel opened the door. A very short, fat man with black disheveled hair and long drooping mustaches was standing before an enormous woman, beating time with a baton while she sang in a nervous, badly pitched soprano voice.

One look at Professor Sollini and Emmy's picture of him as a possibility for Arabel shattered with such suddenness that she thought she could almost hear the pieces hit the floor. Short and fat! And *much* too old!

Suddenly, he clapped his hand to his forehead and cried out, "Enough! Enough!" Then tears came into his voice. "I ask you, I plead with you, I implore you! But you do not listen!" He wrung his hands together and then waved them in the air.

Miss Wells's face began to crumple. "Oh, Professor Sollini!" she wailed.

"No, no, no, no, no!" cried Professor Sollini. "I will not have sniveling! Please, go home now. I will hear you again next Thursday." He sighed heavily and turned away with his hand to his forehead in a grand gesture.

Miss Wells passed Arabel and Emmy at the door. She was dabbing at her eyes with her handkerchief. "He's a wonderful man!" she sobbed. "Just wonderful!"

"My goodness!" whispered Emmy, watching the woman go out.

When the door closed, Professor Sollini turned around, looking perfectly composed, and in a calm voice said, "Yes, my friends? You have come to see Professor Sollini?"

Emmy was so surprised by this sudden change of mood that she said, "Oh, my goodness!" again under her breath.

"I've come in answer to your advertisement in yesterday's *Tribune*," said Arabel timidly.

"Ah!" said Professor Sollini. "I have already turned down nine people."

"Oh," said Arabel and turned toward the door, taking this as a dismissal.

"Wait!" called Professor Sollini. "Why are you leaving? You are not going to sing for me? You are not going to show me what you can do?"

"I—I thought—" stammered Arabel.

"Never think! Act!" advised the professor.

Emmy stared at him. What kind of a statement was that when people were always saying, "Think first—then act!"

"Sing!" commanded Professor Sollini.

Arabel looked helplessly at Emmy. "What shall I sing?" she asked the man.

"Anything!" he replied, waving his hand. Then he put it to his forehead and closed his eyes.

" 'Under the Greenwood Tree,' " hissed Emmy.

Arabel clasped her hands together tightly and began to sing, first softly and uncertainly, then, as she relaxed, sweetly, purely. Her voice soared and fell melodiously on the notes of the old song.

Emmy watched Professor Sollini closely to read his expression, but his face was completely immobile. He didn't so much as flicker an eyelash until she had finished. Then he popped his eyes open and said, "Your teaching qualifications?"

Arabel told him.

"Begin tomorrow afternoon at three o'clock. Two hours every Wednesday and Friday afternoons. Good day."

They were on the street before Arabel could say, "He didn't even ask my name!"

"What's more important," said Emmy, "you didn't ask him how much he would pay!"

"Oh, my heavens!" gasped Arabel. "Are you *sure* we're able to take care of ourselves in New York?"

"Sure," said Emmy. "At least you got the job! It's bound to pay something!" She took Arabel's arm and hurried her along the street toward Mrs. Piddleby's. "We have to change our dresses and walk all the way back to Lissa's house by four o'clock!" She took three happy little skips in a row and said, "Oh, Arabel! No clams today!"

In their room, Arabel began hastily to pull out the band-boxes. "Shall I wear my green merino, Emmy? Oh, everything is so mussed! I didn't realize those Piddleby children did so much damage yesterday. Oh, dear!" Arabel sat back on her heels looking upset.

Emmy had pulled out her wine-colored bombazine. It, too, was full of wrinkles. Emmy stood up. "I'll run down and ask Mrs. Piddleby if she will heat a sadiron for us! We'll press both dresses."

"Will we have *time?*" wailed Arabel. "I shouldn't have stopped at Professor Sollini's!"

"Of course you should have! You got the job, didn't you? I'll be right back." And with that, Emmy went tearing down the stairs to the kitchen.

In just a few moments, she was back. "Look at this!" she cried happily, holding aloft two sadirons, one in each hand. "What luck! Mrs. Piddleby is ironing in the kitchen, and she said we could have these two hot ones. She wanted us to bring the dresses downstairs, but I told her we could do them up here."

"Good!" said Arabel. "Here, I'll smooth mine on this side of the bed, and you use the other side."

At last they were washed, brushed, and dressed. "How do I look?" said Arabel, peering into the tiny mirror over the washstand. "I declare, I can only see half my face in this mirror!"

"You look lovely," said Emmy, tying her bonnet. "How do I look?" She turned around for Arabel to see.

"Very pretty," said Arabel. "Now, let's run!"

They left the sadirons with Mrs. Piddleby before they went out and told her they would not be home for tea.

"What a pity!" said Mrs. Piddleby. "We're having clam chowder. It's real special the way I make it, with lots of clams."

"Let's hurry," said Arabel. "We must be right on time."

Halfway to Amity Street, it began to rain. It had been partly cloudy all morning but hadn't looked too threatening up to now.

"Oh, *dear!*" fretted Arabel. She put her hands over her bonnet and broke into a run.

Emmy tried to keep up with her. "We've been running ever since we arrived in New York," she panted. "We never seemed to run so much in Geneva!"

"What can we do? It's too late to go back for an umbrella."

The rain came down harder and harder. Emmy could feel the dampness seeping through her shoes and wetting her stockings. When they reached the corner of Amity Street and Broadway, they stopped under an awning to catch their breath.

"Look at that clock," said Emmy. "Now we're going to be early, after all that rushing."

Arabel brushed the rain off her cloak and smoothed her hair. "It's a good thing. We'll just stay here a few minutes and collect ourselves. We don't want to arrive wind-blown and breathless. What would strangers think of us?"

Fortunately, the rain lessened while they waited, although it was too late to prevent Emmy's feet from being damp and uncomfortable.

They found Lissa's house, and promptly at four o'clock they walked up the stone steps and rang the bell.

A rosy, shiny-cheeked girl in a crisp white apron and cap answered the door and dropped a curtsy. "Come in, ma'am."

"We are Arabel and Emmy Thatcher," said Arabel.

The maid took their cloaks. "Yes, ma'am, you're expected. Miss Abbie is in the back parlor."

But before she could show them down the hall, Lissa came running out to greet them. "I'm so glad you've come! When it began to rain, we were afraid you wouldn't." She called to the maid. "Kitty, Aunt Abbie says you may bring in the tea now, when it's ready."

Emmy looked around her as they went down the hall. The walls were paneled walnut with a handsome stairway going up, and on the floor there was a beautiful rich green carpet with bouquets of flowers in it.

The back parlor was even more elegant. It was all rich carpeting and carved mahogany furniture and great gold-framed, pier-glass mirrors. And the colors were so lovely! Pale, dusty-pink walls, rich wine-colored velvet on the furniture, soft rose in the rug. And for an accent, a fine black and jade-green satin stripe on the side chairs. Emmy sighed with admiration.

"Aunt Abbie, Uncle Bramble, these are my new friends, Miss Arabel Thatcher and Emmy Thatcher." A pretty, brown-haired woman with fine, clear gray eyes came forward smiling warmly and holding out her hand.

"I am so happy you could come. Do sit down, my dears."

Mr. Bramble was a huge man with side whiskers and a tremendous mustache that covered half his face. He had nice twinkly eyes, and he bowed low to both girls, saying something that was obviously cordial but coming through all those whiskers sounded somewhat like "Bumble, bumble, bumble."

Lissa threw them a merry look and said, "Uncle Bramble is very happy to meet you."

"Oh," said Emmy and smiled at Mr. Bramble.

Kitty came in with the tea things, and Aunt Abbie began to pour. "Lissa tells me you are from upstate," she said to Arabel.

"Yes, Geneva," replied Arabel.

"And you like New York?"

"It's exciting! Of course, it's very different from Geneva."

"Of course," smiled Aunt Abbie, "but it only takes getting used to."

Mr. Bramble leaned forward in his friendly way and said something Arabel couldn't quite catch. At her puzzled expression, Aunt Abbie stepped in smoothly with "Mr. Bramble understands you are the new teacher at Miss Fenwick's?"

"Oh, yes," replied Arabel. "I teach music, rhetoric, and spelling."

Mr. Bramble made another remark that seemed to get lost in his whiskers, and Aunt Abbie smiled. "Yes, very

accomplished," she said. "Lissa tells us you sing beautifully."

"Oh, my," said Arabel, flushing. "No. I'm afraid Lissa
has exaggerated."

"Have some of Trippey's raisin cake?" Lissa started to
pass the plate of thickly sliced cake to Emmy. "Or would
you like bread and butter and brown sugar, first? Or perhaps some of these hot mince tarts?"

The water was running in Emmy's mouth at just the
sight of such a fine assortment of good things on the tea
table.

Just as she was starting to say that she would have some
bread and butter and brown sugar first, Aunt Abbie broke
in. "Oh, you must have some of these first, Emmy. They're
quite a delicacy." She took the silver cover off a round
china dish and passed it to Emmy.

Emmy stared at the bowl, and then shot Aunt Abbie an
apprehensive look. "Wh-what are they, Miss Spenlow?"

"Pickled clams, my dear. They're delicious."

"Yes, do try them, Emmy. They're good," urged Lissa.
And even Mr. Bramble gave her a big encouraging nod.

Emmy glanced swiftly at Arabel who was looking at
her with a tense, worried expression. Emmy straightened
up, swallowed hard, and took two clams on her plate.
Pickled! While the others resumed chatting, Emmy stared
at the curled-up objects on her tea plate. If she sat there
all afternoon, she was sure she could never bring herself
to put one in her mouth. She looked longingly at the plates
of cake and mince tarts and bread and butter.

Suddenly, Mr. Bramble began speaking to Aunt Abbie in a low voice, and that lady said, "Oh, yes, Thornwell, that would be delightful. You *will* sing for us when we've had our tea, won't you, Miss Thatcher? Oh, you must. We should love it! Would you like to see what music we have? Come with me for a moment." Aunt Abbie opened the big sliding doors that joined the back parlor with the front parlor and went to the piano in search of the music.

Mr. Bramble said something to Lissa, and she replied, "Oh, yes, Uncle Bramble. I'll call Kitty for more hot water." And she went out into the hall.

Instantly, Mr. Bramble rose, crossed to Emmy swiftly, took her plate, tossed the two clams into the fire, gave her a clean plate, and passed her the hot mince tarts.

When the others came back into the room, Mr. Bramble and Emmy were smiling at each other like very old friends, and Emmy was halfway through her first mince tart. By the time Lissa's grandfather arrived, Emmy had had three slices of bread and butter, two of layer cake, and a second mince tart! She was deliciously full and had forgotten all about those horrid pickled clams.

Mr. Spenlow was a fine ruddy-cheeked old man with snow-white hair and side whiskers and piercing blue eyes.

"Ah, yes. The Misses Thatcher," he said kindly, shaking hands with them both. He shook his head at Aunt Abbie. "No, Abigail, I've had my tea. I was detained at the shipyard."

"More trouble, Father?" said Aunt Abbie.

"No, no. Just interruptions. By-the-by, Abigail, Dan'l

McWhinney sent his man Jethro over this afternoon with two tickets for Jenny Lind's concert Wednesday evening. Dan'l and Mrs. McWhinney have both come down with colds and congestion. Can't possibly go. Most everyone we know has tickets, but he wanted me to give them to *some-one*, so they wouldn't go to waste."

"Oh, Grandfather! Miss Thatcher and Emmy could go! They don't have tickets!"

Arabel's face brightened instantly, but she said, "Oh, I'm sure you must have friends who could use them."

Aunt Abbie laughed. "I don't know of a single, solitary acquaintance of ours who is not going to be there! It is the most remarkable thing how Mr. Barnum has stirred up interest in this concert. People talk of nothing else."

"By all means, do use these tickets, Miss Thatcher." Mr. Spenlow took them out of his coat pocket. "I wouldn't want them wasted."

When it was time to go home, it was raining again, and Mr. Spenlow had the carriage brought around to drive them home.

"Really, we can walk it nicely," Emmy told him, but Mr. Spenlow wouldn't hear of it.

"Charlie will have you there in no time," Lissa told them. "Charlie is a duly elected Volunteer Fireman, and he is very responsible."

Just as Emmy began to wonder why a Volunteer Fire-man was going to drive them home, Lissa added, "Charlie is Trippey's son, and when he isn't serving as a fireman, he works for us."

"Isn't this just *elegant?*" whispered Emmy delightedly as they sat back in the comfortable carriage and were whisked through the traffic to White Street. "And it was such a delicious tea, and we're going to hear Jenny Lind—"

"Emmy," said Arabel. "Did you really eat those awful clams?"

Emmy giggled. "What happened to those clams," said she, "is a secret between Mr. Bramble and me *forever!*"

5

JENNY LIND

MR. SPENLOW insisted on calling for Arabel and Emmy the night of Jenny Lind's concert, too. "Bramble is calling for Abigail, of course," he had said. "And that leaves Lissa and me. If you don't come with us, we shall, like as not, rattle all over the carriage, with so much emptiness." And his blue eyes had twinkled in so friendly a manner, there was no refusing. Not that Arabel or Emmy *wanted* to refuse!

"It seems so much to accept, though," said Arabel. "They were so kind in giving us the tickets—and now calling for us. I don't know how we can ever repay them."

"I'm sure they don't want to be repaid," said Emmy.

"That isn't the point," replied her sister. "One must always repay obligations." Arabel was fastening a spray of flowers in her hair. "Oh, dear. Do you think this is going to look all right? I do wish we had something more dressy to wear tonight. I understand everyone is dressing in their finest evening clothes."

"We're not," said Emmy carelessly and then ran over and gave Arabel a hug. "You look just lovely, and evening dresses or no, there won't be anyone prettier than you." And she gave her another hug. These things seemed to matter so much more to Arabel.

"I'll wear my black lace mitts, and this blue pair has drawn up so—I'm sure they will fit you. Do try them on, Emmy."

"They're perfect!" said Emmy, holding her hands out to admire the mitts. "It will dress up my dark blue poplin, won't it?"

They were ready and waiting when the Spenlow carriage drew up outside.

Lissa and Mr. Spenlow greeted them gaily. "They say the Castle Garden doors have been open since five o'clock!" said Lissa excitedly.

"But doesn't the performance begin at eight?" asked Arabel.

"Yes, but Grandfather says six thousand tickets have been sold, and the people have been arriving since the doors opened."

"Perfect nonsense, all this hysteria," grumbled Mr. Spenlow. "No doubt Miss Lind has a good voice, but the city has simply gone out of its senses! There were cheering crowds lining Broadway from Canal Street to Chambers Street the day she arrived."

"And every day since, there have been parades and celebrations," put in Lissa excitedly. "And the Firemen serenaded her in a beautiful program the first night she arrived! Charlie told me all about it! Afterwards Mr. Barnum led her out on the balcony of the Irving House, and she bowed and kissed her hands to everybody and—well, Charlie said she was just wonderful."

"Um-m-mph!" was old Mr. Spenlow's comment.

When they approached the vicinity of Castle Garden, they entered a perfect sea of carriages. Charlie maneuvered their carriage smartly but, in the end, Mr. Spenlow and the girls had to get out and walk some distance to the Castle Garden doors.

"All this confusion," complained Mr. Spenlow. "Perfect nonsense!"

"Oh, look!" Emmy cried. In the waters of the bay surrounding Castle Garden there were hundreds of Whitehall boats filled with people who had come to hear what they could of the concert. The sound would undoubtedly carry through the many windows.

Throngs of fashionably dressed people were crowding in the doors.

Emmy was so fascinated with all the people and the fine jewels and the lights and elegance of the building that she must have been standing open-mouthed because Arabel nudged her and said under her breath, "Don't stare! And close your mouth!"

Emmy popped her mouth shut and grinned apologetically.

"Your seats aren't far from ours," said Mr. Spenlow. "Two rows down and to the left. After the performance, we shall wait for you at the end of our aisle. In this crowd anyone can become separated from his party!"

Emmy couldn't have enough of looking at the great

circular auditorium, ablaze with lights and packed with richly dressed people. "Oh, look, Arabel!" whispered Emmy. From the balcony, in a position directly opposite from the stage, was suspended a gigantic bank of flowers in which was spelled out WELCOME, SWEET WARBLER.

"I've never seen anything like it!" said Arabel. "They've never had anything like *this* in Geneva!" and she giggled at the thought.

"You could put everybody in Geneva in this auditorium and still have room, I guess," added Emmy.

"I wonder who that man is over there, standing in front of that red-velvet armchair! The one under the sign that says A-1?"

The elderly woman sitting next to Arabel overheard this last remark and turned to her, observing her for a moment through her lorgnette. Then she said, "That *person,* my dear, is Genin, the Hatter!" She pronounced his name as if it were something very distasteful on her tongue. "He paid two hundred and twenty-five dollars for that seat, and he is trying to make a spectacle of himself." She sniffed disdainfully. "Tradesmen!"

Emmy nudged Arabel and whispered in her ear, "I guess she wouldn't have spoken to you if she had known Uncle Ben is a farmer!"

A half hour later, the orchestra took its place on the stage and soon began the overture. When it was finished, Signor Bellini sang an aria. At its close, the audience strained forward in excitement. Presently, they saw the musical director coming forward through the orchestra, leading Miss Lind by the hand. The Swedish singer was beautifully dressed in an enchanting gown of white watered silk, trimmed with wide flounces of white lace.

With a great roar of welcome, the vast audience rose to its feet. Emmy jumped up and down, trying to see over the heads of the people in front of her, but all she saw were waving hands and handkerchiefs. The shouting and applause were deafening, and Emmy thought they would never end.

When the noise and cheering finally died away, Jenny Lind bowed in a deep curtsy. The director held up his baton to the orchestra, Jenny Lind clasped her hands loosely, and a breathless hush fell over the audience as the beautiful notes of the "Casta Diva" from Bellini's opera *Norma* poured forth in the greatest purity and sweetness. When she had finished, another great ovation took place. All about her, Emmy heard cries of "Incomparable!" "Angelic!" "Entrancing!"

Arabel's face was aglow with excitement. "Oh, Emmy darling, did you ever hear anything so beautiful as her voice?"

Jenny Lind sang a duet with Signor Bellini and the "Prize Song" which had been written especially for her first concert in America, but the selection Emmy liked best was the "Echo Song." This was a Norwegian cowgirl song, and Emmy thought it was lovelier than any other she had ever heard.

When the concert was over, the audience roared its approval so heartily and so long that Miss Lind finally went backstage and brought out the beaming Mr. Barnum. He then announced that Miss Lind had donated all of her share of the night's concert to various charities of New York, including a handsome sum to the Volunteer Firemen, who had serenaded her on her arrival in New York.

"My ears are just ringing!" Emmy told Arabel on their way up the aisle to meet the Spenlows. "I never heard so much cheering and shouting in my whole life!"

"Wasn't she wonderful!" squealed Lissa. "Just wait 'til I tell Charlie about the gift to the Volunteer Firemen!"

"A very generous gesture," admitted Mr. Spenlow. "I venture to say New York will not soon forget her."

"Oh! Mr. Spenlow!" trilled a voice behind them. "*How* do you *do!*"

Lissa groaned. "Miss Clarenda Jeffers," she whispered to Emmy. "That awful put-on I told you about—the one who wants to marry Cousin Andy."

"And what news have you heard from our Captain Andy?" she said, flirting her fan and looking coy. "He will be home in another few weeks, won't he? I can't *wait* to have him back."

"What does she mean *our* Captain Andy?" muttered Lissa.

Mr. Spenlow replied they were expecting Andy back in time for Aunt Abbie's wedding in November or December. Then, as Miss Jeffers looked at Arabel with lifted inquiring eyebrows, he introduced them.

"From Geneva?" said Miss Jeffers. "Delightful country,

Switzerland. How you must miss its charming landscape."

"Geneva, *New York*," said Arabel, flushing a little.

"*Oh*," said Miss Jeffers, making Geneva, New York, sound even smaller than it was. "I don't believe I've ever heard of it." It became quite clear that if *she* had never heard of it, it plainly was not worth hearing about at all.

"Miss Thatcher is our new teacher at Miss Fenwick's," said Lissa, "and she sings so *pretty!*"

"Does she?" Miss Jeffers smiled coolly and turned back to Mr. Spenlow. "Wasn't her 'Casta Diva' exquisite? Of course, you know, I really consider that *my* song! It's been in my repertoire so long." And she laughed self-consciously, still flirting her fan.

"And I've heard her repertoire too many times!" muttered Lissa's grandfather as they made their way out. Lissa squeezed his arm and giggled. Grandfather never minded saying what *he* thought, she told Emmy.

After the concert, Mr. Spenlow took the girls to a late supper at Delmonico's, a fashionable and exclusive restaurant on South William Street, where they were joined by Aunt Abbie and Mr. Bramble.

Arabel was very quiet throughout the supper, and Emmy guessed it was because she didn't feel well dressed or too sure of herself in so wealthy an atmosphere. Emmy herself was fascinated with all the red velvet and cushiony carpets and snowy tablecloths and sparkling silver. And the menu! She didn't know there were so many different dishes in the entire world. She and Arabel had let Mr. Spenlow suggest, and they had quickly assented. The only thing that awed Emmy was the amount of silver beside her plate, but by watching Aunt Abbie closely, she managed to pick up the right fork at the right time.

When they were back in their attic room at Mrs. Piddleby's, Emmy flopped on the bed and said dreamily, "Did we ever, *ever* have such a perfectly elegant, wonderful time in our entire lives?"

But Arabel didn't answer. She was standing in the middle of the floor with a far-off look in her pretty dark eyes, and Emmy wasn't sure it was a happy look.

"What's the matter, Arabel? Didn't you have a good time?"

Arabel gave a little start. "Oh, yes, Emmy. Yes, I had a good time."

"What were you thinking about so hard?"

Arabel hesitated a moment. "Oh, I was just wondering what Lissa's cousin Andy is like." She looked a little embarrassed after she said it. "They all talk about him so much," she explained with a little laugh.

"I can't wait to meet him," said Emmy, watching her sister. "He must be terribly exciting!"

Arabel began to brush her hair so that Emmy could no longer see her face. "He'll probably be a disappointment," said Arabel lightly.

"How can you say that?" demanded Emmy. "When Lissa says he is handsome and dashing and brave and—"

Arabel put her brush down abruptly. "I don't want to meet him!" she said and began to braid her hair with deft, swift fingers.

70

Emmy just stared at her. "You don't want to meet him?" Well, if *that* wasn't stubborn! "*Why not?*"

Arabel finished her braid and tied a narrow ribbon around it to hold the end. "I don't know," she said slowly, and there was a little droop to her shoulders.

After they were in bed, Emmy lay awake a few moments thinking. She must really try to find some work to help out, too. Arabel's salary at Miss Fenwick's was very small because part of it went for Emmy's tuition. They had to be very careful about everything. It was why they had only tea every night and did without a real supper. And Arabel would never be able to buy a new dress at this rate—and the old ones couldn't last forever. Well, come tomorrow, she'd see what she could do.

The next afternoon while Arabel went to the Select Music Academy to teach for Professor Sollini, Emmy went straight home with her books and then right out again. She had decided to go down Broadway and inquire in all the stores whether or not they needed a willing girl as a helper after school.

She was full of hope and courage until she came to Broadway, but as she began to walk past the stores, her enthusiasm dwindled. The stores looked so full and busy that she imagined the shopkeepers would not want to bother with her, or else the stores were too empty and she was afraid they would say they had no need for her.

At last, she came to a thread store. Peeking inside, she saw one customer toward the rear and a kindly looking old lady behind the counter in the front. Emmy gathered up her courage and went in.

"Yes, child?" said the old lady. "You want some thread? Do you have a sample to match?"

"N-no," replied Emmy. "I—that is—" She hesitated.

"Yes?" encouraged the old lady, peering over the counter at Emmy.

"I wanted to ask, do you need a very willing girl to help out after school every day?"

The old lady regarded her gravely for a moment. "Yourself?"

"Yes, ma'am," said Emmy. "I can do a lot of things, and I could come every afternoon."

"It's odd you should have come in," said the old lady. "I was just saying to my sister Adelia that we need someone to sort the spools of thread every day." She leaned over a little closer. "Customers mix them up, you know," she said and nodded and winked at Emmy.

"I could sort thread," said Emmy.

"It isn't a big job," said the old lady. "Perhaps a half hour every afternoon. It would only be a pennyworth of work a day."

A penny! Emmy's enthusiasm sank. Still, a penny was better than nothing. "I'll come tomorrow, if it's all right," she said.

The old lady nodded and winked again. "What's your name, child?"

"Emmy Thatcher, ma'am."

"Very well, Emmy. I'm Miss Serena, and I'll expect you tomorrow."

It's a beginning, Emmy told herself, walking on down the street. When she came to the button store, she gathered her courage and went in, but the proprietor was brusque and told her they had all the help they needed. She passed the pastry store and the bootmaker and the dry-goods store. None of them had looked inviting. Besides, she didn't think there would be anything she could do to help in them.

As she came to a corner, she heard music down the side street and turned to see what it was. There was a group of five men all blowing some kind of brass horn, and the tune was gay and lively. Children were dancing around to the music, and passers-by had stopped to listen. Emmy walked down the street to see them. When they had finished the tune, a man threw them a coin. One musician caught it neatly in his hat, and they began to play again.

Turning back toward Broadway, Emmy passed a greengrocer's. Inside, sitting on a pile of cabbages, was a large gray cat. He regarded Emmy gravely from his lofty seat and then closed one eye halfway in what looked like a deliberate wink. Emmy chuckled. That ought to be a good omen! She continued down the block with a lighter heart.

At a delicatessen the smells were so tantalizing that Emmy stopped to look in the window. Large pans of potato salad with parsley topping, strings of sausages, hoops of cheese, and small barrels of pickles crowded the shelves. There was a big pot of baked lentils and wurst in one corner and beside it—beside it, was a small sign! *Girl Wanted* it said. Underneath in smaller letters it said *part-time only.*

"Well!" said Emmy and went right in. She addressed the man behind the counter. "May I speak to the proprietor, please?"

"You vant to speak mit who?" The man looked puzzled.

"The proprietor," repeated Emmy. Then she added, "The owner. I'd like to speak to the man who owns this store, please."

The man's face brightened. "Ach, ja. The *owner*. That's *me!*"

"Oh," said Emmy. "Well, I saw your sign in the window, and I'd like to ask about it."

"Ja? Vot sign in the vindow? Something you vant to buy, ja?"

"No," said Emmy. "The sign that says *Girl Wanted*."

"Oh," replied the man. He rubbed his chin and stared at her a minute.

"Please, sir, I can do a lot of things," Emmy hurried to assure him.

"So?" said the man. "Such a little girl?"

Emmy straightened up to her full height. "I'm not little," she protested. "And I'd like a job very, very much."

"Hm-m-m," murmured the man, beginning to smile.

"You look a little like my Elsa used to look when she was your age."

Emmy smiled back. "Your daughter?"

He nodded. "Ja. She's married now and lives in Philadelphia yet." He looked Emmy over again. "It's only a little job—like the sign says."

"Oh, that's all right," said Emmy hastily. "I go to school half the day."

"I don't know, though." He frowned and hesitated. "It could be dangerous if it should be you don't know how to handle a knife right."

"I can handle a knife!"

"Vell, vat it iss," explained the man, "iss parsley-chopping."

"Parsley-chopping?" said Emmy in surprise.

"Ja, parsley-chopping. It takes time, you know? My vife now, she iss very busy home with the salads and the baked lentils and the other things—" He waved his hand around. "And vell, my vife don't *like* to chop parsley. She says to me, 'Hans Hoffelmeier'—that's my name—'Hans Hoffelmeier,' she says, 'I do everything else, but I *don't chop the parsley!*' She says to me, '*You chop it!*'"

Emmy was grinning up at him. He had a round, jolly face and a big, wide mustache.

"Now, I got no time to chop parsley. I got to tend to the customers. You see, liebchen?"

Emmy was looking happier all the time. "*I* can chop parsley, Mr. Hoffelmeier."

"Ja?" said Mr. Hoffelmeier. "Well, now maybe you can.

76

Maybe you can. Two, three girls came in already, but they not interested in such a little job, you know?"

"*I* am, Mr. Hoffelmeier."

"I can't pay much for such a little job. It takes maybe fifteen minutes every day. No more."

Emmy's face fell.

"But maybe you could chop onions, too? My vife don't like to chop onions neither. That's maybe another fifteen minutes. Half an hour in all." He looked at Emmy. "That's better, no, liebchen?"

"How—how much will you pay, Mr. Hoffelmeier?"

"Vell, for half an hour's chopping—" He hesitated and rubbed his chin again. "Five cents, liebchen, that's all it's worth."

"Every day?"

"Ja, every day. Only not Sunday, of course."

Thirty cents. Together with the six cents from the thread store, that would be thirty-six cents a week. Well, that wasn't bad!

"Thank you, Mr. Hoffelmeier, I'd like to have the job."

"Ja? That's good. Very good." He leaned across the counter and said confidentially, "I had to chop the parsley my own self this morning. Ja! So you see you come just in time, liebchen."

"Shall I start tomorrow?"

"Ja, tomorrow. You be here at eight o'clock? Ve got to start the salads early."

"Are you open earlier, Mr. Hoffelmeier? I have to be

at school promptly at nine, and I have to walk all the way to Eighth Street with my sister and—"

"Ach!" said Mr. Hoffelmeier. "Ve are open at seven o'clock."

"Then, could I come at seven-thirty?"

"Ja, that vill be fine. And, liebchen," he called as Emmy started for the door, "I include maybe a roll and some wurst for your lunch every day, too, ja?"

Emmy threw him a bright smile. "Thank you, Mr. Hoffelmeier. Thank you very much."

She went out the door and down the street with such a bubbling feeling inside that it was hard to walk without skipping! She had two real jobs, and the thirty-six cents would help out, too. She couldn't wait to tell Arabel!

6

THE INVITATION

NOVEMBER was cold and damp. The Franklin stove in Arabel's and Emmy's room heated well enough as long as it was going, but there never seemed to be enough coal for it.

"I just hate to keep asking Mrs. Piddleby for more coal," sighed Arabel.

"But the room is without heat all day long!" Emmy was bundled up in a jacket, a coat, and her heavy wool scarf. "And it takes a while to warm it after we get home, and then it doesn't last until bedtime. She ought to give us more coal!"

"Let's don't make too big a fuss over it," warned Arabel. "The rent for these lodgings is really very reasonable, and what would we do if we had to look for something else? Everything else would be much dearer."

Emmy sighed in agreement. Then she had a sudden happy thought. "Oh, Arabel, look what Mr. Hoffelmeier gave me this morning! A whole cheese and this lovely loaf of rye bread—*and* two pickles! There, now. We don't *have* to eat clams today, *do* we?"

"Oh, Emmy, I can hardly bear the sight of a clam any more, either! But it's a lovely cheese. Why don't we go down for tea and then for once be able to have a little supper—up here in our room."

Emmy considered this. It would be nice not to go to bed with that empty feeling. "All right, let's!"

Mrs. Piddleby welcomed them as usual. "Well, well, good afternoon, girls. Sit right down. Tea is all ready. Nat, move over there."

Arabel and Emmy spoke to everyone as usual and as usual received no response except head-bobbing and grinning from Nat and Mr. Piddleby (they hadn't heard the sound of their two voices, yet) and giggling from the three little girls.

But Mrs. Piddleby made up for the others' silence. "Well, it's been a fine, bracing day, hasn't it? A *little* on the warm side, of course."

"*Warm!* It's been so *cold* today, Mrs. Piddleby," protested Emmy. "It's awfully cold! We can hardly get our room comfortable!"

"Oh, my. Your blood must be thin," said Mrs. Piddleby. "Why, I've had the kitchen windows open all day." And indeed she looked warm with her ruddy, glowing face and her sleeves rolled up above her elbows.

"It's terribly unhealthy to have a house too warm. My, yes. Then, when you go out, you take your death of cold from the change. My, yes."

Arabel and Emmy exchanged glances. There was no use going on with the discussion, for Mrs. Piddleby plainly did not think they needed more coal than she gave them.

"Here's the tea." She set the large teapot on the table. "And here are the crackers and here is the horse-radish, fresh grated—" She was looking very pleased with herself and acting as if she had a special treat for them. Emmy's heart sank. She was very apprehensive about Mrs. Piddleby's treats.

"I'll bet you didn't expect *this!*" said Mrs. Piddleby and triumphantly brought in an enormous platter of raw clams and set it in the middle of the round table. "It was so warm today, I thought it was the perfect time to have them!"

Raw clams! Emmy stared at them in unqualified horror! This was positively, absolutely, the last straw! She took one more quick look at the wet, gray-looking things and hastily rose from the table.

"I—I—" she began, swallowed, and went on. "I feel a little ill, Mrs. Piddleby. I hope you will excuse me. I really can't eat anything this evening."

Arabel jumped up, too. "Oh, Emmy darling! You do look a little green." She turned to Mrs. Piddleby. "I'll go up with her. If we could just take our cups of tea with us—perhaps she will be able to drink a little of it after a while."

"But aren't *you* going to have any of these lovely clams?" Mrs. Piddleby looked very disappointed. The others weren't much concerned, being very occupied with cramming the raw clams into their mouths, which Emmy vowed later they swallowed whole!

"No, thank you, really. You see we had such a large lunch. It's probably what has caused the trouble." It wasn't true at all, but anything to get Emmy away from the clams.

Back in their room, the two girls collapsed with laughter. Once well away from the sight of the raw clams, it seemed very funny—particularly since they had the bread and cheese tucked away in the chest of drawers.

"Quick, before the tea gets cold!" said Arabel, and they

sat down to the best tea they had had since their last visit with the Spenlows.

"Lissa says her Aunt Abbie's wedding is planned for the end of this month if her cousin Andy gets back with the *Dauntless*," said Emmy, chewing on a good crust of rye bread.

"And if he's delayed?"

"They'll just wait. But Lissa says he and the *Dauntless* understand each other, and they'll manage to get here."

Arabel smiled. "Isn't it amazing how seamen feel about their ships?"

"I guess they feel the ship is almost human, after a while. Mr. Spenlow told Lissa the *Dauntless* would do anything for Andy."

Arabel gave a little shiver. "It almost makes you feel creepy."

"I think it's romantic," said Emmy. "I wish I were a boy! I'd go to sea!"

Arabel looked at her sister with teasing eyes. "Think of all the clams you might have to eat!"

Emmy groaned. "I never thought of that!"

They ate in silence for a moment, and then Emmy remembered. "Oh, I forgot to tell you. Lissa and her Aunt Abbie have asked us to tea again tomorrow."

Arabel set down her teacup and frowned. "Emmy, we *can't* go on accepting tea at Miss Spenlow's when we have no means of returning it."

"Why, Arabel!" began Emmy.

But Arabel shook her head. "You know we *cannot* have

them here. The entire house smells eternally of clams, and we *couldn't* bring them up here in this small room with only one chair. The front parlor is absolutely the Piddlebys', and they've never even offered it to us. We certainly can't entertain the Spenlows in the kitchen, and so far as I can see, there's no way of returning their kindness."

Emmy's face was as long as the bedpost. "You mean we can't go there any more when it's so much fun and so cozy and they have such *delicious* teas and they're all so very nice—"

Arabel looked miserable, too. "You know how particular one has to be about returning courtesies."

"I know, but—"

"There can be no buts," said Arabel. "I'm just as sorry as you are, but we've been to tea at the Spenlows' on an average of once a week since we met them, and it's got to stop."

Emmy sighed heavily and began to help clear away the bread and cheese. "Let's leave this cheese out tonight," she said. "It's going to make everything in this drawer smell of it." She chuckled. "It will be as bad as my hands every day. To save my life, I can't get all the smell off after chopping those onions for Mr. Hoffelmeier."

The last week in November, Lissa came to school bubbling with excitement. She ran over to where Emmy was hanging up her cloak and threw her arms around her, almost knocking her off her feet.

"Guess what! Guess what!" she cried, forgetting to keep her voice down.

"What?" said Emmy.

"Cousin Andy and the *Dauntless* came in on yesterday afternoon's tide! Oh, isn't it thrilling! I'm so *happy!* And it was a record run, and Grandfather is very proud of him and Aunt Abbie is so glad because now she can go ahead with the wedding and *ooooh!*" She gave a joyous little squeal and swung Emmy around again.

"I'm so *glad!*" Emmy told her, hugging her back. "But, Lissa, don't talk so loud. Miss Fenwick will be here in a minute, and she'll give you a forfeit mark!"

"I don't *care!*" announced Lissa. "Nothing could make me feel bad today!"

At lunch recess, Lissa talked about nothing but Cousin Andy and the *Dauntless*. "And they ran into this dreadful typhoon rounding the Cape and a seaman was lost overboard and Cousin Andy put back to look for him and sure enough he was clinging to a cask he had been carrying when he was washed overboard and Cousin Andy tied a rope around his waist and went in after him and the waves tossed him all about but finally he managed to reach the man and they were both hauled aboard." She finished breathless.

"Oh, my!" said Emmy admiringly.

"And we wouldn't have known about it at all if Grandfather hadn't read it in the ship's log. Everything has to be entered in the log, you know."

"He must be very brave!" said Emmy.

Lissa looked proud. "Oh, my, yes! And oh, I was almost forgetting. Here is a note for your sister from Aunt Abbie. It's an invitation, I think. There will be a lot of parties now until the wedding next month." Lissa sighed importantly. "Oh, it's going to be rush, rush, rush! And did I tell you I am going to be Aunt Abbie's bridesmaid? Won't it be simply thrilling?"

Emmy nodded, starry-eyed. She couldn't imagine anything more exciting! She had never been to a wedding herself.

"Come home with me after school," said Lissa. "I'll show you the dress material Miss Dilliker is going to make my bridesmaid's dress of."

"Oh, I can't, Lissa," explained Emmy. "I have to sort thread at Miss Serena's."

When school was dismissed, Emmy and Arabel hurried home together. This was an afternoon when Arabel taught for Professor Sollini. There was a cold, piercing wind, and they walked with their heads bowed and cloaks drawn close around them. "Can't you open Miss Spenlow's note now?" begged Emmy impatiently.

"Not in this w-w-wind!" Arabel's teeth were chattering.

"But Lissa said it was an invitation, she was sure."

"Oh, dear," said Arabel.

"We'll meet Lissa's cousin Andy at last! Won't it be exciting?"

Arabel groaned softly. "I wish we didn't have to accept this invitation—whatever it is!"

"Why, Arabel!" Emmy was shocked.

"I don't care. It's the way I feel."

It didn't sound like Arabel at all, and Emmy stole a glance at her sister's face. It looked pale and pinched from the cold. She was thinner, too, than she had been when they came to New York three months ago. She still looked pretty, though. Emmy guessed there wasn't anyone prettier than Arabel.

In their room, Arabel started the coal fire, and they stood over it rubbing their hands and holding them out for the first warmth from the stove.

Emmy hugged her cloak around her. "Do you suppose the North Pole is any colder than this?"

Arabel grinned wryly. "I wouldn't want to find out," she said.

Presently, when the fire had caught on well, she reached in her pocket for the note from Aunt Abbie. It *was* an invitation. Old Mr. Spenlow was giving a dinner party for Aunt Abbie and Mr. Bramble in honor of their approaching wedding in December. The invitation included Emmy, too. Since Lissa was a member of the wedding party, she had been allowed to ask Emmy and Dodie.

"Oh, Arabel!" said Emmy excitedly, throwing her arms around her sister. "A real dinner party!"

But Arabel didn't look so happy. "What will we *wear?*" she said in a worried voice.

"Well, you've got your green merino, and I have my wine-colored bombazine."

"Oh, Emmy! Those aren't party dresses! This is going to be a formal dinner! The Spenlows are wealthy, and

87

everybody will be dressed beautifully, I know. You saw how people looked at Jenny Lind's concert."

Emmy looked sober. It was true. The others would be dressed in beautiful clothes and . . . But on the other hand, they just *had* to go! "Couldn't we make something over?" Aunt Hannah had always made over their clothes.

"*What?*" said Arabel.

They both thought this over for a minute.

"My brown satinet isn't too bad," said Arabel. "But the bodice won't do at all. If I just had a bit of fabric to make a new bodice, I might—" She looked off, frowning.

"Don't we have anything we could use?" asked Emmy.

Arabel shook her head. "Not a thing—except that pretty length of brown lace Aunt Hannah gave me. You remember Cousin Frances gave it to her, but Aunt Hannah hates brown."

"Of course." Emmy began to brighten up. "Now, all you need is a piece of fabric to make a new bodice."

Arabel looked more cheerful, too. "Perhaps, if it had a wide neckline, I could put the lace all around it like a bertha—"

"And very short sleeves so the bertha would fall over the edge," said Emmy.

"Perhaps a gray—no, a pale blue. That would be pretty with the brown." Then she sighed. "I might as well forget it, Emmy. I was doing sums last night after you were asleep, and we have only enough money to meet this month's expenses and send a little to Aunt Hannah and Uncle Ben to pay on our debt."

Emmy said, "Hadn't you better hurry? You're due at Professor Sollini's at three o'clock."

Arabel jumped up. "Oh, heavens! What am I thinking of?" She snatched up her cloak and bonnet. "I'll be back as soon as I'm through!" She ran down the stairs, tying her bonnet strings as she went.

Emmy closed the door and, stooping down, pulled out her bandbox. She felt down in one corner underneath her old gray cashmere. There it was. She pulled out a knotted handkerchief and sat down on the bed. Opening it carefully, she spread out the contents. She counted slowly, two dollars and twenty-two cents, two dollars and fifty-eight cents, two dollars and ninety-four cents. There! She had made it all by herself with the thread sorting and the parsley- and onion-chopping. Arabel had insisted she save every penny of it to spend on herself, but now Emmy gathered it up happily and put it in her little drawstring reticule.

A short while later, while she was sorting thread for Miss Serena and while there was no one in the store, she asked the old lady a question. "Miss Serena, where would be a good place to buy enough satinet to make a bodice?"

Miss Serena cocked her head and thought a minute. "For yourself?" she said.

"No, for my sister. She has a brown satinet skirt, and if she had some more fabric, she could make a new bodice with some lace she has, and it would be like a new dress."

Miss Serena nodded. "Certainly. And a very smart thing

to do, too. I always make over my dresses. Now, I don't suppose you want to pay too much for it?"

"No," said Emmy. Then she added quickly, "But I want a *nice* piece."

"Well, you go right down the street to Mr. Jackerly's. You tell him Miss Serena sent you. He'll give you a nice piece of material, and he won't overcharge you, either." She winked and bobbed her head at Emmy.

Later, coming home from Mr. Jackerly's store with a lovely piece of pale blue satinet wrapped in a neat bundle under her arm, Emmy couldn't think when she had felt happier. The fabric had been reasonable enough, and there was a nice jingle from the remaining money in her reticule. She was impatient to see Arabel's face when she showed her her surprise!

Arabel was unusually long in returning from Professor Sollini's. Emmy had been peering out the window for some time and feeling a little worried when she at last heard Arabel's footstep on the stairs. She ran to meet her sister at the door.

"What kept you so long?" said Emmy.

Arabel threw off her cloak and bonnet and ran to the stove to warm herself. "Oh! It's cold outside." She shivered. "And the wind is even stronger! I'm sorry I'm late. I had a little errand to do. Look!" Arabel took a bundle from inside her cloak and opened it. It was a length of dark wine cloth with a gay print of tiny flowers in yellow, pink, and blue.

"Oh!" said Emmy, her heart going right out to it. "How

90

adorable, Arabel! Where did you get it? And what is it for?"

"I got it for you, Emmy. It was in the window of a shop on my way to Professor Sollini's. I thought if I made an overskirt of this for your wine-colored bombazine and took out the sleeves just for the party and put in some puffy ones made of this print—well, wouldn't it do for the dinner party?"

"Oh, Arabel!" Emmy threw her arms around her sister and gave her a mammoth hug. "And what are you going to wear?"

"Well, now, there's no use being silly about this. I'll just wear my green merino, and maybe I can drape the ivory shawl around it, the one that used to be Mother's."

"But it won't look like a party dress!"

"It doesn't matter," said Arabel.

Emmy ran across the room and took her package out of the chest where she had hidden it. "See what *I* bought for *you!*"

Arabel just sat and stared at the package a moment.

"Open it!" Emmy was almost dancing up and down with excitement.

Arabel gave a little squeal of astonishment when she saw the pretty blue satinet. "Oh, Emmy! Enough for a new bodice! *Where* did you get it?"

"I bought it with my very own money!" declared Emmy proudly.

"But I wanted you to *keep* every penny of that!"

"Pooh!" said Emmy, sounding like her friend Lissa. "Do you like it?"

"It's perfect! Oh, Emmy, I'm so happy."

"And while we're talking about it," said Emmy, "where did you get the money to buy this print for *me?*"

"Oh, I—I—that is, I had a little extra money tucked away."

Emmy shook her finger at her sister accusingly. "I happen to know that all the money you could have had tucked away was the money to buy our lunches with."

"Oh, I only used half of it—" Arabel blurted out and then clapped her hand over her mouth.

"*Your* half?" demanded Emmy.

"Well, I'm getting too plump anyway," Arabel defended herself.

Emmy gave her sister another big hug. "Mr. Hoffelmeier gives me such an enormous roll and wurst every day, it's enough for both of us."

Arabel laughed and hugged her, too. "But we'll have to have our tea with Mrs. Piddleby for the rest of the month!"

"I don't care!" said Emmy gaily. "I'll get those clams down—just as long as they aren't raw! And I think it's going to be too cold for that."

• 7 •

"AND THE PARTY IS TOMORROW"

As soon as class was dismissed for lunch, Lissa ran over with her lunch basket to sit beside Emmy. She was bubbling with excitement.

"Trippey has the entire house upset with her cleaning and polishing and waxing! Grandfather is threatening to go live at his club until it's all over," giggled Lissa. "And such *delicious* smells have been coming from the kitchen for days! Trippey won't even let me in, she's so busy. Not that I would be in the way."

Emmy sighed happily. "And the party is tomorrow."

Lissa munched away on bread and butter and a chicken leg. "M-m-m," she nodded. She paused and frowned. "That Clarenda Jeffers is going to be there! Grandfather wasn't going to ask her at all, but Cousin Jennifer insisted and, well, Aunt Abbie said perhaps he'd better."

"I remember we met her the night of Jenny Lind's concert."

"The reason Cousin Jennifer wanted her to come is because she and Clarenda Jeffers are best friends, and Cousin Jennifer thinks Clarenda would make a perfect wife for

Cousin Andy!" Lissa scowled at the thought. "Imagine that prissy old Clarenda Jeffers married to Cousin Andy!" Lissa looked stormy just thinking of it!

Emmy couldn't help laughing. "And what does your cousin Andy think of it?"

At that, Lissa grinned, too. "Cousin Andy and I are perfectly agreed on Miss Jeffers," she said with satisfaction. Then she smiled and moved closer to Emmy so the others couldn't hear. "I'm so eager to have Cousin Andy meet your sister," she said confidentially. "I just love her, and she is so very pretty! And Grandfather says so, too, and so does Aunt Abbie and Uncle Bramble."

Emmy glowed at Lissa's praise of Arabel.

"I've been thinking—wouldn't it be nice if they liked each other?" Lissa went on enthusiastically. "Why, if they got married, you and I would be practically sisters!"

Although Emmy had been secretly thinking the same thing, she didn't want to admit it so soon. "Oh, Lissa!" she laughed. "They haven't even met yet!"

But Lissa wasn't to be laughed down. "Well, you have to help these things along. Now, if it hadn't been for me, Aunt Abbie and Uncle Bramble might not be engaged right now!"

"*What?*" said Emmy, not knowing whether Lissa was serious or not.

"It's true," said Lissa stoutly. "I did it with a golden walnut."

Emmy's mouth fell open in surprise. "Is that—is that a riddle?"

Lissa giggled delightedly and gave Emmy a little hug. "Never mind, I'll tell you about it sometime. But right now, let's plan a little about your sister and Cousin Andy. I saw the seating arrangement on Aunt Abbie's desk this morning. She has made a little plan, and your sister was seated next to Mr. Jollifer, and Cousin Andy was next to Mrs. Millard."

"You wouldn't dare!" whispered Emmy, thinking of the same thing herself.

"I certainly would!" declared Lissa. "And I will. The last thing, after everyone has arrived, I'll slip down and change the cards around so Cousin Andy will sit next to your sister."

"But someone will notice! Your Aunt Abbie—"

"Pooh!" scoffed Lissa. "It will be too late, then. Aunt Abbie would never say anything after people were seated."

The next day was bright and cold. Emmy got up early, as usual, and ate a hasty breakfast of tea and bread and butter (after refusing the clam stew). On her way to Mr. Hoffelmeier's she half ran to keep warm.

"Good morning, liebchen! Good morning," he greeted her cheerily. "You are out of breath, ja?"

Emmy grinned as she tied on the big apron Mr. Hoffelmeier kept for her. "I ran!"

"So? Vell, it *iss* cold this morning. Ve better have extra parsley and onions today. Cold veather makes for appetite, you know? And ve sell lots of salad and lentils today, I bet you."

Emmy held a bunch of parsley in her left hand and with

an even up-and-down motion worked away at it. After it was minced, she sliced the onions into the great wooden bowl and chopped them with the onion-chopper. She held her head back as far as she could, away from the bowl, but she cried anyway.

"I just wish I knew a way to chop onions without crying," she told Mr. Hoffelmeier, with a rueful grin.

"Ja, liebchen, I know. That's vhy my vife don't like to do it. She says she cries, and then her nose gets red!" He chuckled.

When Emmy was ready to go, Mr. Hoffelmeier came out from the back of the store and said, "Wait, liebchen. It's so cold out—come, have a little coffee and stollen with me. It vill varm you inside."

"I've never drunk coffee," Emmy told him.

"So? Vell, then maybe ve make it all milk and a little hot coffee to varm it up, ja?"

Emmy bit into the coffeecake. "M-m-m," she said appreciatively. It was delicious! The milk with coffee was good, too.

"Ja, it's good, no?" said Mr. Hoffelmeier, taking a slice, too. "My vife baked it yesterday. Ve always have it near Christmas time, just like ve have pfeffernuss and springerle and—"

"What's that?" said Emmy.

"Cookies. Christmas cookies."

"My Aunt Hannah always makes gingerbread cookies at Christmas time."

"Ja," said Mr. Hoffelmeier. "Gingerbread cookies iss

good, too." He regarded Emmy gravely for a moment. "You and your sister going home for Christmas, ja?"

Emmy sighed a little. "No, it takes too much money. The train, you know," she explained.

"Ja," said Mr. Hoffelmeier. "Vell, New York is a very gay place to be at Christmas time, ja! Here, liebchen. I fix your roll and wurst, and I put in some more stollen, too. It makes dessert, no?"

"Thank you, Mr. Hoffelmeier. And thank you for the coffee and stollen." She dropped him a little curtsy.

Mr. Hoffelmeier beamed at her and then bowed very formally from the waist. "Just like my little Elsa used to do," he said fondly. "Good-by, liebchen. I see you tomorrow, no?"

Emmy was just going out the door when she put her head back in to say, "Ja, Mr. Hoffelmeier."

She could hear him chuckling as she closed the door.

After school that afternoon, Arabel and Emmy walked hurriedly toward Broadway. Arabel had to go to Professor Sollini's to teach, while Emmy must hurry down to Miss Serena's thread shop. "Couldn't you have gotten off today?" asked Emmy.

"The only concession he would make was to let me come a half hour earlier," said Arabel. "So, I'll be home shortly after four-thirty."

Emmy left her at the corner of Houston Street and hurried on to the thread shop.

"My, I'm glad you're here, dear," Miss Serena greeted her. "We've had a sale today, and everything is in the

greatest confusion! Could you spend a little extra time sorting, Emmy?"

Emmy had wanted to go home early, but she could see that Miss Serena really needed her. Not only were the colors all mixed up, but some had come undone from so much handling and threads were loose and tangled. Each one had to be carefully wound back and secured. She set to work busily.

It was almost four-thirty as Emmy turned into White Street. She took a deep breath of the cold fresh air and then held it as she opened Mrs. Piddleby's front door. If she ran up the stairs very fast, she could almost make it to the attic floor before she had to take another breath. At that distance, the smell of clams wasn't quite so strong.

As she put her hand to the bedroom doorknob, Emmy thought she heard a muffled giggle. She opened the door quickly and found the three little Piddleby girls in the middle of the room trying on her and Arabel's made-over dresses!

"Beenie!" cried Emmy, horrified. "Take off my dress this instant! Didn't we tell you to never, never, *never* put on our clothes again? And Dorcas! Put Arabel's dress down this minute! You'll wrinkle it holding it that way!"

Dorcas dropped the dress in a heap on the floor and giggled. There was a large smudge where Dorcas had been holding it. Emmy snatched it up. "What is this you've gotten on it?" she demanded. But she didn't have to wait for an answer. Dorcas was eating a slice of bread and molasses! Her sticky fingers were smeared with it.

"Oh, no!" moaned Arabel, coming in at that moment.

The three little girls in a fit of their usual giggles went running out the door and down the stairs.

Arabel didn't touch the dress at first. She just sank down on the bed and burst into tears.

"Don't cry, Arabel! Oh, don't cry!" Emmy ran to her and put her arms around her. "We can wash it off! I know we can!"

"It's not just that. It's everything, I guess! Professor Sollini did nothing but scream at everyone today. He even screamed at me! And I forgot my reticule and had to go back for it in that cold wind, and now this—" She sat up and dried her eyes. "I must be tired," she said, trying to smile. "Let me see my dress."

"I'm sure it will wash off, Arabel," said Emmy.

It did wash off, but it left a discolored circle on the blue fabric.

"Oh, Arabel!" said Emmy sympathetically. Arabel had

worked so hard on the dresses, sitting up late in the cold room and sewing them by hand.

"It's just hopeless," said Arabel. "Look! Right on the left side, *front*. It looks dreadful! I'll just have to wear my green merino."

"No, no," said Emmy, scrambling to pull out the band-boxes. "We can put something over the spot. Here, how about this brown velvet flower on my bonnet?"

"Oh, I couldn't! That's your best bonnet!"

"Pooh!" said Emmy. She snipped off the flower with the scissors and held it over the spot before Arabel could say another word. "There! It's all covered."

"Why, it is! And oh, Emmy, I believe it looks better with the flower!"

They were ready and waiting when Mr. Spenlow's carriage called for them. "You look just beautiful, Arabel!" whispered Emmy as they stood in the hall. Arabel's heavy dark hair was piled high on her head, with soft little ringlets about her face, and her dress was most becoming with its fall of brown lace over the blue.

"It was kind of Mr. Spenlow to send the carriage for us," murmured Arabel as they were being driven to Amity Street.

"He insisted no one was going to use it," said Emmy.

Arabel shook her head and smiled. "He's such a nice man. I wonder if Captain Andy is like him?"

8

CAPTAIN ANDY

THERE were several carriages ahead of them as they reached Lissa's house. Emmy peered out the carriage window to see the guests entering the Spenlows'.

"What a beautiful cloak!" whispered Arabel, who was looking out, too.

It was Miss Clarenda Jeffers. Emmy could see her distinctly when she reached the lighted doorway. She was wearing a rich full black-velvet cloak trimmed with gold tassels that swayed as she walked.

Lissa greeted Arabel and Emmy at the door and whisked them off to the second-floor guest room to remove their wraps. Miss Clarenda Jeffers was removing hers, too.

"You've met Miss Thatcher and her sister, Emmy, haven't you, Miss Jeffers?" said Lissa.

Clarenda Jeffers raised her eyebrows and stared at Arabel as if she had never seen her before. Then she gave a little exaggerated start and said, "Oh, but of course! You're the one from that odd little town—oh, dear, what *was* the name?"

"Geneva, *New York*," said Arabel.

Miss Jeffers laughed as though it were some kind of joke. "Yes, that's it. Geneva, *New York!*"

Lissa looked at her belligerently. "What's so funny about Geneva, New York?"

Miss Jeffers smiled at herself in the long mirror, patted her elaborately dressed hair, touched her eyebrows with a delicate finger. Then she turned to Lissa at she swept out. "Don't trouble yourself about it, dear child. You wouldn't understand."

"Oh-h-h!" scowled Lissa. "I can't *stand* her! She's so—"

"Never mind, Lissa," said Arabel. "It wasn't important."

Aunt Abbie met them at the foot of the stairs as they came down. "I'm so glad you could come!" she greeted them. "How lovely you look, Miss Thatcher."

"Please call me Arabel," said Emmy's sister. "I wanted to ask you to before but—"

Aunt Abbie smiled warmly as she tucked her arm through Arabel's. "I'd love to call you Arabel. Come! I want you to meet our other guests."

"I've got to run downstairs to the dining room and change the you-know-whats!" whispered Lissa and left Emmy to go with her aunt.

Mr. Bramble, looking handsome in his dinner clothes, gave them a low bow and a big, whiskery smile. Old Mr. Spenlow greeted them cordially, and Aunt Abbie moved among the guests with them, making introductions as she went. Emmy's eyes swept the room to find Lissa's cousin Andy, but there were so many people and she was so busy curtsying and saying "How do you do" that she was almost startled when she heard Aunt Abbie saying, "And may I present my nephew, Captain Andrew Spenlow? Andy, this is Miss Thatcher and her sister, Emmy, the new friends we've told you about."

Emmy gave a little sigh and a quick look at Arabel as Andy bowed to them both. Even Arabel would have to admit he was handsome! He had dark hair, and clear gray eyes, like Aunt Abbie, except that Andy's lashes were straight and thick and black. He was still healthily tanned from his recent voyage, but most attractive of all, Emmy decided, was his flashing smile, gay, half-teasing—the kind of smile he was giving Arabel this very minute.

"Oh, yes. I've heard a great deal about you since my return." He stood looking down at Arabel, still smiling as if he were thinking of something very delightful indeed. "You know, you don't look at all like a school teacher," he said, shaking his head.

Emmy giggled and looked at Arabel, expecting to see her smile, too, but Arabel flushed and said rather coolly, "And how did you expect a school teacher to look, Captain Spenlow?"

Well, for goodness' sake! What was the matter with Arabel?

Captain Andy was still smiling, though. "Like Miss Fenwick, perhaps?"

Before Arabel could answer, Clarenda Jeffers came in from the hall and swept across the room to Andy's side. For a fleeting moment, Emmy wondered what Miss Jeffers had been doing in the hall for so long.

Miss Jeffers took Andy's arm in a possessive way and trilled, "Oh, I see you've met Abbie's new little friends! You'll simply *never* guess the *absurd* mistake I made when *I* first met them! My dear, they said they were from *Geneva,* and of course I naturally thought they meant *the* Geneva, but can you *imagine*—they meant—"

Emmy closed her eyes tight. If she heard Geneva, *New York,* said like that just one more time!

Arabel's chin went up. When Miss Jeffers had finished with a ladylike laugh and a tap of her fan on Andy's arm, Arabel said crisply, "Apparently, Miss Jeffers has traveled more extensively in Europe than she has in New York State or she would be familiar with Geneva, *New York.*" Then, as Aunt Abbie came back with other guests, Arabel said, "Please excuse me," and she turned away to meet them.

Lissa came up with Dodie. "I'd have been right back, but Dodie just came. Let's sit over here on this sofa until dinner is announced." She gave Emmy an important wink to show her she had accomplished what she went downstairs for.

Emmy chuckled. Well, she hoped it would be all right. She wasn't sure at the moment that Arabel and Captain Andy were going to get along too well. She looked across the room at Arabel. Her face was still a little flushed, and there was a sparkle in her eyes that looked like anger to Emmy. A little distance away, Andy was looking at her, too, with a half-smiling, half-thoughtful expression.

"Look at that old Clarenda Jeffers hanging on Cousin Andy's arm that way!" fumed Lissa.

"Mama says Miss Jeffers can talk more than any other three people she knows," said Dodie.

"And say less!" snapped Lissa.

Presently, dinner was announced, and the assembled guests made their way down the stairs to the dining room. Lissa, Dodie, and Emmy were seated side by side toward one end of the long table. Lissa nudged Emmy, and they watched as the others found their place cards and took their seats. With a gasp, Lissa said, "Look!"

Clarenda Jeffers was smiling up at Captain Andy and pointing to her place card and then to his. They were seated next to each other!

"*No!*" hissed Lissa. "No, no, no! I changed those cards myself, and Cousin Andy is seated beside your sister!"

But Andy was inspecting both cards, too. He nodded to Miss Jeffers and pulled out her chair.

"Somebody else changed them again!" said Lissa. "*Who?*"

Then Emmy remembered something. "I saw Miss Jeffers coming in from the hall while we were being introduced, a little while after you had come back from—from you-know-where."

"She wouldn't *dare!*" stormed Lissa.

Emmy began to laugh. "*You* did!"

Dodie said crossly, "What are you both talking about?" She didn't like to be left out of a secret.

"I'll tell you after a while," whispered Lissa.

Mr. Jollifer was seating Arabel, directly across the table from Andy and Miss Jeffers. Andy was watching Arabel, but Arabel didn't seem to see him at all. She was smiling in her pretty way and carrying on a lively conversation with Mr. Jollifer.

Lissa was still frowning as she watched them. "*Something* has gone wrong," she said.

After dinner, the guests returned upstairs. The front and back parlors had been thrown together into one long room, and now groups were seating themselves on sofas and in armchairs, chatting gaily the way people do who have been plenteously fed while surrounded by good company.

Dodie yawned discreetly behind her hand. "These late parties," she said importantly.

"Grandfather wasn't going to let me stay up," said Lissa. "But Aunt Abbie said nonsense; after all I was a member of the wedding party! Would you like to come up and see my bridesmaid's dress?"

They trotted happily upstairs and spent a half hour admiring the pale yellow dress with its tiers of matching lace.

"It looks just like a buttercup!" sighed Emmy, holding it up in front of her at the mirror to see how she would look in it. The yellow color was becoming to her, too, with her dark hair and eyes.

"Aren't you scared?" said Dodie. "Imagine walking down the church aisle with all those people watching you!"

"Won't it be *fun?*" Lissa whirled around once on her toes, looking happy at just the thought.

When they went back downstairs, Mr. Jollifer was just sitting down at the piano. Aunt Abbie and Mr. Bramble were talking to him, and Emmy could hear Aunt Abbie saying, "Oh, thank you, Jeremy. You are always so willing! I want to ask Miss Thatch—"

She was interrupted by Clarenda Jeffers who came rushing up. "You dear man," she chided Mr. Jollifer. "Don't be so bashful about asking me. You know I'm always ready to do my part on a festive occasion like this! I haven't my music, but what shall it be?"

Aunt Abbie and Mr. Bramble exchanged surprised glances. Mr. Jollifer looked at Aunt Abbie with an uncertain expression.

"Later," said Aunt Abbie, tactfully. "Do sing, Clarenda." She and Mr. Bramble took their seats beside the other guests.

Emmy looked around for Arabel. Oh, there she was, seated with the Mallows. Arabel was settling back now to listen. Emmy couldn't tell what she was thinking, her face was so immobile. There was Captain Andy, standing by the mantel on the other side of the room. Emmy decided *he* looked resigned.

Miss Jeffers swished her full velvet skirts around her until the folds fell just right, then she assumed an artificial pose, and took a deep breath. She nodded to Mr. Jollifer.

Lissa groaned under her breath.

Miss Jeffers sang with much eyebrow-lifting and many gestures. Of all things, she was singing "Casta Diva," the aria Jenny Lind had sung so beautifully at the concert.

"Will you listen to what she's singing?" demanded Lissa, still whispering. Then she subsided into silence because she caught Aunt Abbie's warning glance from across the room.

Miss Jeffers made her mouth into an affected letter "O" when she sang, and the tones came out quite loud but not musically at all, Emmy thought.

There was a polite round of applause when she had finished. Before anything could be said, she nodded to Mr. Jollifer again and plunged into a second song. Old Mr. Spenlow put an end to it, then, by going over to the piano and thanking Miss Jeffers for her singing. He seated her firmly between Mr. and Mr. Jefferson, and then came over and held out his hand to Arabel.

"We have another talented young lady with us this evening. You will sing for us, too, won't you, my dear?"

Arabel was so taken by surprise that Emmy could see she didn't know what to say for a moment.

Aunt Abbie said, "Yes, *do*, Arabel! *Please* do."

Arabel didn't want to sing, Emmy could tell, but in spite of it, she rose with dignity and took her place beside the piano. Arabel didn't think people should hang back and make spectacles of themselves when asked to perform. Emmy hoped she wouldn't be nervous. Arabel looked a little pale now but very, very pretty. She spoke with Mr. Jollifer a moment, and then he began to play "Robin Adair."

A complete hush fell over the room. Arabel stood quietly, her soft dark hair shining in the candlelight, and her face turned toward Aunt Abbie and Mr. Bramble.

The notes of the old song came out purely, sweetly, delicately, as she sang. Mr. Jollifer was enchanted and looked up at Arabel's face more often than he looked at the keyboard.

Across the room, Captain Andy was still standing beside the mantel. There was just the hint of a smile around the corners of his mouth and some other expression in his eyes that Emmy couldn't quite define.

There was a tremendous burst of applause and demands for more.

"The old songs!" said Mr. Spenlow. "The old songs are the ones I love! Sing another, my dear."

Arabel flushed prettily at all the enthusiasm. Emmy could see she was surprised that everyone had liked her

song so much. Arabel and Mr. Jollifer conferred again, and she began to sing "Gather Ye Rosebuds While Ye May."

Old Mr. Spenlow closed his eyes and nodded his head gently in time with the music, a happy expression on his face.

Andy stood motionless throughout the song, but when it had ended, he made his way across the room to Lissa and whispered in her ear. She grinned up at him and promptly ran over to Arabel at the piano.

Arabel listened as Lissa spoke to her, then she turned and glanced quickly in Andy's direction. He flashed a quick, mischievous smile at her, and Emmy was sure Arabel was getting pink again.

Mr. Jollifer played the introduction, and Arabel began to sing ever so sweetly, ever so tenderly, "How Shall I Your True Love Know" but with never a look in Andy's direction.

When the evening was over, Arabel and Emmy thanked Mr. Spenlow and Aunt Abbie and hugged Lissa and said good-by to Mr. Bramble. Miss Clarenda Jeffers was saying good-by just behind them.

"You sang charmingly, my dear," old Mr. Spenlow told Arabel.

"Those simple old songs are quite refreshing, aren't they?" said Miss Jeffers, overhearing. "I've never felt they were worth bothering with, myself, but *some* people still like them."

Andy was nearest the door. "I enjoyed your singing

very much indeed, Miss Thatcher. And I didn't mean what I said about teachers the way it sounded. I really meant to say I never expect teachers to be so pretty!"

Arabel flushed again, but she looked straight into his gray eyes and said evenly, "No apologies are necessary, Captain Spenlow. Good night."

As they were going down the steps, they could hear Clarenda Jeffers' affected voice behind them. "*Dear* Captain Andy, we shall see you tomorrow at the Warrens'? Isn't it *delightful* to have all these prenuptial parties for dear Abbie and Mr. Bramble?"

"That Clarenda Jeffers!" fretted Emmy. "Lissa is right. She is a hateful old—"

"Hush!" commanded Arabel. "It isn't important."

Emmy thought it must have been a little important though, because she was almost sure there was a hint of tears in Arabel's voice.

9

THE DAUNTLESS

AND THE wedding is to be on the twentieth of December, and Miss Spenlow and Mr. Bramble have asked me to sing." Arabel was reading a note from Aunt Abbie.

"Oh, Arabel! What fun!" Emmy was delighted. "That means we are both invited to the wedding!" She paused a moment at Arabel's downcast expression. "What's the matter? Don't you want to sing at the wedding?"

"Oh, yes," Arabel assured her. She shivered a little and looked toward the Franklin stove. "Do you think we dare put another lump of coal in? We have only five lumps left."

Their room, as usual, was cold and drafty. They were sitting with their feet as close to the stove as they could get them. There was a howling snowstorm outside, and Arabel and Emmy had stuffed strips of an old petticoat all around the windows, but it was still cold.

"If worst comes to worst, do you think we could burn the washstand in this stove?" asked Emmy.

Arabel chuckled a little at her sister's joke and then sighed heavily. "Do you know, Emmy, I've had a ridiculous hope that we might see Aunt Hannah and Uncle Ben for Christmas?"

"They're coming *here?*" cried Emmy. She had tried not to think of Christmas being so close when she knew she and Arabel were going to spend it alone.

"No, no," Arabel hastened to say. "That's just it. Here's a letter from Aunt Hannah. It's so odd, because she says they had hoped all fall to be able to send us our train fare to Geneva and back as a Christmas gift, but Uncle Ben has had some bad luck. The last windstorm blew part of the roof off the barn, and of course that had to be mended immediately and so . . ." Arabel's voice trailed off, and she put the letter down.

"Wouldn't that have been wonderful?" said Emmy wistfully. Then she pulled herself up short and said in a lively voice, because she could see Arabel felt sad and depressed, "Well, never mind. As Mr. Hoffelmeier said the other morning, New York is a very gay place to be at Christmas time!" Emmy paused and sniffed the air. "Do you suppose the Piddlebys will have clams for Christmas dinner?"

"That's another thing. Mrs. Piddleby told me this morning that she and her husband and the children are going to her sister's for Christmas Eve and Christmas Day. They won't be home until late that night. So we'll have to look after our own meals those two days."

"Oh, that's all right!" said Emmy.

"She said she would be glad to leave extra clams for us."

"Oh, no, Arabel! *Anything* would be better than that!"

Suddenly, they both began to giggle. It was all so ridiculous! Clams, clams, clams! No one would believe them even if they told about the Piddlebys and their clams—not that they wanted to tell anyone.

"Miss Thatcher! Miss Thatcher!" Mrs. Piddleby was shouting up the stairs. "There's somebody here to see you!"

Arabel jumped in surprise. "What—? Who could it be?" She got up quickly and opened the door. "Thank you, Mrs. Piddleby. I'll be right down!" She turned to Emmy nervously. "Who could it be? No one we know ever comes here." She smoothed her hair and then the flounces of her dress. "Come with me," she begged Emmy.

They went down the stairs together. As they reached the landing overlooking the vestibule, Arabel gasped. Standing in the hall below was Andy, dusting the snow from his hat into Mrs. Piddleby's umbrella stand.

"Oh, Emmy!" whispered Arabel, looking as if she were going to run back up the stairs.

Emmy caught her arm. "Come on!" she said. "It's all right!"

Captain Andy looked up and saw them then. He smiled at sight of the two girls and said gaily, "I feel just like a snowman! I hope I haven't disturbed you."

"Oh, no," said Arabel and under her breath to Emmy, "Where can we ask him to sit down?"

But Captain Andy settled her fears by saying, "I just stopped in for a moment to deliver a message from Aunt Abbie. If the wind drops by this afternoon, will you both join us in a skating party? We're going out to a lake on the Bloomingdale road."

Skating was something Arabel and Emmy both loved and something they did well. Arabel's face lit up for a moment, and then she said, "Oh, I'm so sorry, but we didn't bring our skates with us when we came to New York." She laughed a little. "I guess we didn't think we would be skating in the city."

"Aunt Abbie thought you might not have yours with you. She said to tell you she has several extra pairs."

A door opened down the hall toward the kitchen, and a strong odor of cooking clams swirled into the hall. Andy sniffed.

There was also the sound of giggling behind the front parlor door. Those Piddleby children again! They were standing behind the door, probably looking through the keyhole as Emmy had caught them doing several times. Andy hear it, too, for he looked in the direction of the parlor door, and the corners of his mouth twitched a little.

Arabel moved nervously toward the front door and opened it for Andy. "Thank you so much for stopping by with the invitation," said she.

"And if the weather is suitable, we may call for you about three this afternoon?"

Arabel started to say yes, when the voice of Samuel Snacker, the other clam man, broke in on them. "The clams I want to sell today! The best of clams from Rockaway!" He was coming up White Street, closer and closer to the Piddleby house.

"Oh, my goodness!" murmured Emmy. If they could

only get Andy out of the house before Mrs. Piddleby heard the clam man!

"Yes, yes, thank you," Arabel told Andy hurriedly, almost pushing him out the door.

But it wasn't soon enough. With a rattle and a bang, Mrs. Piddleby came storming out the rear hall door with a large pail of steaming water. "Where is he? Where is he?" she screamed. "I know I heard him!"

Andy stepped back in astonishment as Mrs. Piddleby hurtled by, sloshing him a bit with the hot water. "Where are you, Sam Snacker?" she shouted. "Didn't I tell you to stay off this block? Didn't I? Didn't I?"

Outside, the clam man was shaking his fist at Mrs. Piddleby. "You can't tell me where to sell my clams! This is a free country, ain't it?"

"I'll free country you!" screamed Mrs. Piddleby in a frenzy and, taking a big swing with the pail, threw the hot water in the direction of Samuel Snacker.

"I'll get the leather heads! That's w'ot!" he yelped, running down the street. "Police! Police!"

"He'll get the leather heads! Pagh!" cried Mrs. Piddleby, turning back and shaking her finger at Andy. "He knows he can't sell those no-good clams in our block! I've told him before and I'll tell him again! None of his clams in this block! No, sir! Not as long as my Ebenezer is in the clam business, no sir!"

Arabel stood frozen with embarrassment, but Emmy like Andy was struggling to keep a straight face. As soon as Mrs. Piddleby had disappeared down the hall again,

Emmy and Andy burst into a gale of laughter. But not Arabel! She turned and went flying up the stairs without another word.

Andy stopped laughing when he could and looked after Arabel's retreating figure. "I'm sorry," he told Emmy, taking out his handkerchief and wiping his eyes. "But it was funny. I'm afraid your sister didn't feel that way, though." He put on his hat. "We'll hope to see you this afternoon. Lissa is looking forward to showing you where she skates."

Upstairs, Emmy found Arabel collapsed in a heap on the bed, in tears.

"Oh, Arabel! What's the matter now?"

"Nothing!" Arabel's voice came muffled and teary.

"It wasn't as bad as all that," Emmy consoled her. "Captain Andy thought it was funny!"

Arabel sat up, and her eyes snapped. "Funny! *Ridiculous*, you mean! And *we* looked ridiculous! What can he think of us? Living here in this house full of clams and all that giggling behind the parlor door and no place to ask him to sit down and then that awful scene with Mrs. Piddleby and the clam man and she sloshed hot water on Captain Andy's boots and—oh-h-h!" Arabel dissolved into tears again.

Emmy stood looking at her, feeling very, very puzzled. This didn't seem like Arabel. "Why would all that make *us* look ridiculous?" she asked sensibly. "We didn't do anything."

"Oh-h-h!" sobbed Arabel again.

Emmy sat down on the little cane-bottomed rocker and

studied her sister a moment. "Arabel," she said, "is it because you like Captain Andy so much?"

Arabel sat up again. "Certainly *not!*" she said, with too much emphasis, Emmy thought. "Certainly not. Why should I like him? All he does is stand around and—and—laugh at a person!"

"Why, Arabel! He doesn't at all. It's just that he has such a twinkly smile. I think it's friendly!" Emmy smiled herself, thinking of it. "I *like* him! And don't you think he's *handsome?*"

"Oh-h, *handsome*. What difference does that make?" And Arabel dabbed at her eyes with her handkerchief again.

"But, Arabel—Lissa and I were hoping you and Captain Andy would like each other and—" Emmy blurted out before she thought.

"Well, you just needn't!" said Arabel, sounding tearful again. "I don't have any time for foolishness! It's all I can do to please Miss Fenwick and Professor Sollini and try to make a go of it this year. I don't see how we can go back to Geneva when there wasn't enough work for me at Mrs. Hudley's School and Aunt Hannah and Uncle Ben have it hard enough as it is and need the money I am paying back. We just *have* to make our way here." She wiped her eyes again. "And I've no business going to a lot of social affairs I can't keep up with, either! I don't have the clothes, and everyone can see I'm just a country school teacher and—" She went off into tears again.

Emmy was beginning to feel worried. She didn't know

what to say, so she went over to Arabel and hugged her. After a while, Arabel sat up and said that Emmy should forget what she had said. She was just feeling tired.

But when the weather cleared and Captain Andy and Lissa came for them, Arabel said she had a dreadful headache and couldn't go. No amount of coaxing would change her mind, and Emmy went down without her.

Aunt Abbie and Mr. Bramble expressed regret as well as Andy. It was a shame for Arabel to miss the fun, thought Emmy, as the five of them drove briskly out the Bloomingdale road in a sleigh, with all the bells ringing musically. At the lake, they found a large crowd already enjoying the season's first skating.

"Isn't it wonderful?" said Lissa happily. "I can't remember when we've had skating so early!"

"It won't last, Lissa, my girl," warned Andy, skating around them in a large lazy figure eight.

"But there's bound to be more," Lissa told him. "This is only the beginning!"

"Come on," said Andy. "Let's do a circle chain!"

"What is it?" asked Emmy.

"You'll see. Here, take my right arm. Lissa, take my left."

The two girls each took an arm, and the three of them went skating down the lake together. "Now, hold on!" said Andy, and he suddenly whirled them around and around while he stayed in one spot. In a moment he stopped them, and they skated on a few yards where he whirled them around and around again.

"Whee!" Lissa screamed delightedly.

"Ooooh!" squealed Emmy, not sure she was going to keep on her feet each time.

"He won't let you fall!" shouted Lissa. "Whee!"

When they had spun around again and again, Andy finally came to a halt and said to Emmy, "Look!"

Behind them, where they had been skating and whirling, was a perfect chain of circles cut in the ice.

"It was fun!" said the girls. "Let's do it again!"

"No!" groaned Andy. "Once is enough! But I'll race you around the lake!"

Of course, they never caught up with him even though he would wait until they were tantalizingly close before he started off again.

"I've never seen so many people skating all at once!" said Emmy later when they were resting.

She looked about her at the crowds on the ice. Young and old alike were whizzing around at varying speeds on the fine smooth surface. There were even several quite elderly ladies seated in chairs equipped with runners being pushed by younger companions on skates.

Richly dressed folk in velvets and furs mingled with poorer citizens in worn and patched woolens, all brought together by their mutual liking for the pleasures of skating.

Emmy and Lissa held hands as they glided smoothly again around the lake.

"I'm so sorry your sister couldn't come," said Lissa. "Cousin Andy was disappointed, I think." She gave Emmy a mischievous little wink. "Do you think your sister likes

Cousin Andy? I was so mad to think our plans went wrong the night of the dinner party!"

Emmy looked solemn. "I don't know, Lissa. She seems so upset this last week. Ever since the dinner party, come to think of it. I don't know *what* she's thinking."

"Tsk!" said Lissa. "These things just have to be helped along."

But this was easier said than done, as the next two weeks proved. Arabel made one excuse or another and refused three invitations in a row where she might have seen Andy and had managed to avoid him altogether.

Emmy and Lissa were about to despair when things took a change for the better at the rehearsal two days before the wedding. Arabel and Andy were both there, for Arabel was to sing at the wedding and Andy was to act as best man. There was not much opportunity to talk during the rehearsal, but at the end when they were preparing to leave the church, Andy turned to Arabel and Emmy. "You must let me drive you home," he said. "As you see, it is snowing again."

"How thoughtful of you, Andy dear," said Aunt Abbie. "Thornwell and I have an errand to do downtown. Shall we all meet back at our house for tea?"

"I thought perhaps Miss Thatcher would have tea with me at the Astor House," said Andy, smiling down at Arabel. Then, as she started to shake her head, he added quickly, "Chaperoned by Lissa and Emmy, of course!"

Emmy and Lissa squealed delightedly at the unexpected treat, and Arabel had to say she would. The two girls chattered happily as Charlie maneuvered the carriage skill-fully through the crowded street. Snow drifted lazily down, and the soft blue of early twilight began to settle over the city. Stores were already lighted for the conven-ience of late afternoon shoppers, and there was a cheerful bustle of street cries and voices as well as the usual rumble and clatter of carriage wheels and horses' hooves on the cobblestoned street.

"There's the *Blue Man!*" said Lissa, pointing out the window. "Look! See him? Isn't he odd looking?"

"Where?" said Emmy. Why, there *was* a man who looked blue! Quite blue indeed, his hands and his face, too.

"He's always there near the Herald Building," said Lissa. "They say he was so heavily dosed with some kind of medi-cine once that it turned him blue."

Emmy shook her head in wonder. You could see just about *anything* in New York.

"If this snow keeps up," said Lissa happily, "every car-riage and omnibus will have to change its wheels for run-ners, and then the city becomes almost quiet. Except for the beautiful sound of the sleigh bells, of course."

Emmy glanced at Andy and Arabel. Andy was doing most of the talking as Arabel sat back in one corner, her face almost hidden in the shadow.

On what seemed a sudden impulse, Andy leaned forward and said, "Miss Thatcher, would you by any chance like to stop on South Street for just a moment before it grows dark and see the *Dauntless?* It's my ship, you know."

Arabel hesitated, but Emmy and Lissa set up such a

clamor that Arabel said she would like to see it very much indeed.

Charlie turned the carriage at the next corner and drove across town to South Street. The tang of salt air and tar and spices met them before they saw so much as the spar of the first ship.

"Here we are!" said Andy with a happy ring in his voice. He helped them out and offered his arm to Arabel. Together, they went up the gangplank with Emmy and Lissa following.

The seamen greeted Andy respectfully and touched their caps to the ladies as they came aboard.

"It's beautiful!" breathed Emmy as they stood looking up, up into the tall, straight, square-rigged masts with their bleached sails so neatly furled—then down the beautiful, tapering, immaculate deck. "I've never been on a ship before."

"You haven't?" said Lissa, surprised.

"No ships in Geneva," said Emmy.

Arabel took a deep breath and putting out her hand touched one of the masts. She stood like that a moment, looking up its long length, and Andy smiled. "It's moving a little," she said.

Andy looked up at the mast, and a faraway look came into his gray eyes. "You should see her when her masts are billowing with white sail—when she's cutting into the Pacific with a foamy thrust—when the wind roars in her rigging—"

Arabel sighed a little as he paused.

Lissa was telling Emmy what the sails were called. "And that one up there is the mizzen topsail and that's the main topgallant and that one's the fore royal and that one's the —the—"

"The mizzen skysail," said Andy.

"I always forget that one!" said Lissa crossly. "Anyway *that* one is the flying jib and that one back there is the spanker! And that's only part of them."

They walked around the spotless deck, and then Andy took them inside the captain's cabin. It was richly paneled with satiny walnut and furnished comfortably with a large desk, some chests, and carved walnut chairs. Overhead, an oil lamp was lighted. It threw a wide circle of soft warm light on the carpeted cabin floor and reflected a pattern of little lights on the ceiling through its pierced metal shade. Emmy thought the lamp swayed ever so gently as she looked at it.

"And you sail all the way to China and Malay and the Indies?" said Arabel in a dreamy voice as she looked at the maps on the walls.

"And back," said Andy, and Emmy saw he was smiling.

"And back," said Arabel in a whisper, as if to herself.

It was dark by the time they reached the Astor House. Inside, the lamps were cozy and warm and the round table in a corner just the right size. They all joined in gay and light-hearted chatter while they waited for their tea. Even Arabel seemed a little giddy and laughed musically at Andy's teasing of the two girls. Emmy and Lissa

127

exchanged delighted looks at this change of events. After a little, their tea arrived with lovely little frosted cakes and cinnamon toast and gingernut bars and all manner of delicious tidbits which Emmy didn't recognize.

They were about to finish when someone in a very rustly skirt swept by, paused, and swept back to their table. "But Captain Andy!" trilled the high-pitched voice of Clarenda Jeffers. "You naughty man! I expected to see you at the Neddings' this afternoon! You played truant, now, didn't you?"

Andy rose and bowed to Miss Jeffers.

She looked at Arabel. "Oh, I believe it's Miss—Miss—"

"Thatcher," said Andy distinctly.

"Oh, yes," laughed Miss Jeffers. "Thatcher. I always forget. How do you do?"

Arabel said, rather stiffly, "How do you do."

"I see you are manfully entertaining the out-of-town-ers," said Miss Jeffers.

"It's a pleasure," Andy assured her.

"Of course," said Clarenda Jeffers with another of her affected little laughs. "Well, good-by for the moment. I shall expect you at eight tonight?" And she swept off again.

Andy sat down. "She's giving a dinner for Aunt Abbie and Uncle Bramble tonight," he explained, looking at Arabel uneasily.

Arabel had that withdrawn look again. "There's no reason to explain," she said coolly.

When Andy and Lissa left them at Mrs. Piddleby's, Lissa took the opportunity of whispering in Emmy's ear, "What went wrong *this* time?"

Emmy shrugged helplessly. "*I* don't understand it!" she whispered back.

∞ 10 ∞

TROUBLE FOR CHRISTMAS

ND YOU know how weddings are," Lissa whispered to Emmy as they put their cloaks on after school. "Grandfather says everybody gets sentimental, so we'll see if things take a turn for the better tomorrow."

They were still worrying about Arabel and Andy.

"I wish we could do *something*," continued Lissa, "because Cousin Jennifer is certainly doing everything she can to bring Cousin Andy and that Clarenda Jeffers together!"

Emmy shook her head sadly. "And Arabel won't even talk about Andy. And she's upset all the time. I think it's hopeless."

"Let's keep trying," said Lissa.

Aunt Abbie's wedding was at five o'clock. Emmy, sitting in the velvet-cushioned pew near the front, looked around her and sighed happily. She had always wanted to see a big church wedding, and this was going to be such a lovely one! The church was richly decorated with evergreen boughs and sprays of holly, and the chancel gleamed with tiers of candles. White satin ribbons marked the center aisle and were tied with sprays of holly at each pew.

Mr. Cantrell, the church organist, was playing softly and nodding his head up and down, up and down, as if he were very happy about something.

The ushers were seating the last of the guests. My! The big church was almost full. Emmy turned back in time to see Arabel take her place beside Mr. Cantrell near the chancel and begin to sing. How very beautiful Arabel looked in the candlelight—a little pale perhaps, but still beautiful. Emmy hoped Arabel was warm enough, standing there in her brown and blue satinet frock. True, she had put on every one of her petticoats and a wool chemise besides, but the church was so cold! And Arabel had been coughing a little that morning.

In the row across the aisle, Emmy could see Clarenda Jeffers looking very haughty and disapproving when she saw that it was Arabel who sang. Emmy smiled with satisfaction.

Arabel sang so sweetly and tenderly that Mrs. Mallow was beginning to wipe her eyes, and even Cousin Jennifer was sniffling. Emmy guessed weddings did, indeed, make people feel sentimental.

Now Mr. Cantrell struck the first chords of the wedding march! Everyone rose and looked toward the rear of the church. There was Lissa looking adorable in her pale yellow dress with a yellow nosegay to match. She was coming slowly down the aisle, stepping very carefully in time with the music. Behind her came Aunt Abbie on old

Mr. Spenlow's arm looking radiant and beautiful in the palest dove gray to match her pretty eyes.

They were met at the altar by Mr. Bramble and Andy. Mr. Mulgrove, the minister, opened his prayer book to the marriage service and began to speak. Emmy was enchanted! The twilight had deepened outside and the windows of the church were a deep, dusky blue. Emmy's eyes wandered to the background of evergreens, the masses of holly, the flickering tiers of candles, the hushed guests all looking forward with gentle smiles and a tear here and there.

Lissa, standing to one side, now glanced back and caught Emmy's eye for one fleeting second. Then she looked at Andy. Emmy followed Lissa's gaze quickly and saw that Andy was looking past Aunt Abbie and Uncle Bramble, straight into Arabel's eyes where she stood near the front pew. And she was looking at him, too—all the while the lovely old words were being spoken. There was a pause, and then Mr. Mulgrove nudged Andy who came to with a start and hurriedly felt in his waistcoat pocket for the ring. He had missed his cue! Emmy was sure she saw Lissa chuckle for just an instant, and there was a smile playing around Andy's mouth, too.

When the ceremony was over, they all drove back to Amity Street for the wedding reception. Lissa and Emmy were to ride in the carriage with Arabel and Andy, or at least that was the way Aunt Abbie had suggested it beforehand. However, Lissa had a better idea. "Quick!" she whispered to Emmy. "Let's fix it so Cousin Andy and your sister will ride to Amity Street by themselves. Perhaps it will give them a chance to talk a little. They ought to be feeling nice and sentimental right now!"

Emmy giggled and gave Lissa a little hug. Lissa was so clever! They waited until Arabel had been handed into the carriage, and then Lissa cried, "Oh, Dodie! Wait for us! We have something to tell you!" She turned to Andy who was holding the carriage door and waiting. "You don't mind if Emmy and I ride over with Dodie, do you?"

Andy gave her a quick smile. "If you insist." He bent down and whispered, "And thanks!"

"Honestly!" laughed Lissa as they ran to Dodie's family's carriage. "I can't fool Cousin Andy about anything!"

"Oh, Captain Andy!" trilled a voice Emmy had begun to know well. "Do you have room for one more? Cousin Jennifer is bringing the Neddings, and I am left over!"

"Oh, *no!*" hissed Lissa and Emmy in one breath.

Andy opened the door and got out again to help Clarenda Jeffers into the carriage, and then it drove off.

"Oh-h-h!" fumed Lissa. "She always spoils everything! She did that on purpose, too! I know she did."

"We'd better *give up*," said Emmy, feeling all was lost somehow.

"Never!" said Lissa stoutly. "We'll think of something else!"

But Emmy was beginning to suspect they might do better if they stopped trying to help. Things had a way of turning out in very unexpected fashion!

The Spenlows' house on Amity Street had never had a gayer party than the wedding reception. The house was ablaze with lights, adorned with flowers, and the collation was simply elegant! Trippey had outdone herself. Emmy stood happily eating from her plate, which was loaded with all manner of delicious foods from the immense sideboard.

"Have you had some of these jellied cranberries?" said Lissa.

"I have everything!" Emmy assured her.

Lissa looked her plate over critically. "You don't have any oysters."

Emmy shook her head. Oysters! They looked much too much like clams for Emmy's taste, and they were raw! But Lissa was eating them with enjoyment. Emmy looked away. There was just something about watching people eating raw clams and oysters . . .

"Look at that!" whispered Lissa.

Clarenda Jeffers was still clinging to Andy's arm, although Emmy thought he seemed to be trying to disengage himself. Arabel was across the room carrying on an animated conversation with Mr. Jollifer, who was looking very attentive. Emmy considered Mr. Jollifer a moment. Well, if worst came to worst . . . Of course, he *was* older and getting a little bald—still, he was quite nice and played the piano agreeably.

Emmy's eyes wandered back to Andy, and she sighed. But Andy was so very handsome and exciting and gay! He had a way of making everything so much more fun when he was around. Just then, he turned his dark head away from Miss Jeffers and looked across the room to where Arabel was talking so gaily with Mr. Jollifer. He frowned slightly and turned back to Clarenda Jeffers.

There was going to be dancing later, but in a few minutes Arabel came to Emmy and said, "Do you mind if we go now, Emmy? I feel very tired."

Arabel looked tired, indeed. Her cheeks were flushed, and her eyes were too bright.

They said good-by to Mr. and Mrs. Bramble, both of whom kissed them on the cheek and thanked Arabel again for singing at their wedding ceremony.

Andy came over to ask if he could drive them home, but Miss Jeffers, who was still holding persistently to his arm, said with a pout, "But, Captain Andy! They are just starting to dance, and you promised me!"

"We wouldn't think of it," said Arabel quickly and without looking at Andy. "Mr. Spenlow has been so kind as to call Charlie around with the carriage."

On their way to Mrs. Piddleby's Emmy was sure Arabel was crying. After a little she began to cough again.

"Before we go in, Arabel, we ought to buy some medicine for that cough," Emmy told her. "It sounds worse than it did this morning."

"It's nothing," said her sister. "It's just that I was so chilled standing there in church. I'll feel fine tomorrow."

But Emmy wasn't so sure. She leaned forward and called to Charlie. "Could you please stop at an apothecary's shop so we can buy some medicine for my sister? She has a cough."

"Yes, Miss Emmy," replied Charlie. "How about Mer-

135

cherson's up ahead? And if it's a cough your sister's got, she couldn't do better than buy *Mrs. Jervis's Cold Candy.* Jings, no! She couldn't do better."

Presently, they were safely at Mrs. Piddleby's and with *Mrs. Jervis's Cold Candy* in Emmy's hand.

"You sit down," she told Arabel. "Try to keep warm until I get this fire going. Br-r-r! Seems colder than usual, doesn't it?"

When the fire was well started, they drew up as close as they could get without scorching themselves and Emmy opened the package containing the Cold Candy. "Listen to this," she said, reading from the box:

> "For lungs or throat,
>   No antidote
>   Of half as much real service is
>   For cough or cold
>   Of young or old
>   As that of Mrs. Jervis's."

This struck Arabel so funny that she went off into a fit of laughter, which started her coughing again.

"Here," said Emmy, "take one of these cough candies while I read you what it says on the other side.

> " 'What causes ailments manifold?
>   A cold.
>   What gives the sweetest voice a coarseness?
>   Hoarseness.
>   What spoils a singer's best cadenza?
>   Influenza.

What carries tens of thousands off?

A cough . . .' "

Emmy stopped and looked at Arabel in alarm. Arabel, ill as she was, began to giggle again, which brought on still more coughing.

"No, no, no," gasped Arabel. "It isn't going to carry me off! Don't look so worried, Emmy darling."

But Emmy *was* worried. Arabel looked too flushed, and that cough didn't sound good at all.

By the next morning, Arabel was quite hoarse, but she insisted on getting up and going to church, just as she insisted on going to school when Monday came. "But what difference can it make?" said Emmy. "School will be dismissed for Christmas holidays tomorrow anyway."

"I *must* go," said Arabel in a hoarse whisper. "I can't afford to displease Miss Fenwick right now. You know that."

"But you aren't feeling well!" said Emmy, really alarmed. *Mrs. Jervis's Cold Candy* hadn't helped much— that Emmy could see.

"I'm all right!" said Arabel so crossly that Emmy knew for certain that she wasn't feeling like herself.

By Christmas Eve, Arabel's cold had become so much worse that she didn't get up for breakfast. Mrs. Piddleby sent up a pot of tea, two buttered muffins, and a warning to keep warm and stay in. She was leaving the key to the coalbin on the hall table, and if their room got too cold, they were to take an extra scuttleful of coal because of Arabel's cough.

A few minutes later, the Piddlebys were off for their two days' jaunt, and the house settled into a deep, unnatural quiet. Emmy walked to the window and looked out again. The sky was a cold, sullen, lowering gray that threatened something disagreeable. Christmas Eve! At home in Geneva, Aunt Hannah would be preparing a big fat goose for tomorrow's dinner, and Uncle Ben would be setting up a fine Christmas tree that he himself had cut in the woods that very morning. And if Emmy were there, as she had been these past seven years, why, right now she would be stringing cranberries in long ropes and tying red strings on gingerbread cookies to hang on the tree and—Emmy's eyes misted a little just thinking of all the rich and lovely smells in Aunt Hannah's kitchen and the feeling of love and warmth.

Emmy stared across the street at the row of houses which looked so much alike. In each one, a family was preparing for Christmas. The chimneys were smoking away cheerily, and yes, there was a Christmas tree leaning against a doorway and down the street a housewife was fastening an evergreen wreath to her front door. The woman shivered a bit, looked up at the leaden sky, and then went in and closed the door behind her.

Clop-clopping down the street came the butcher's cart. Fat geese and turkeys were wrapped loosely and piled in baskets. The boy hopped out with one and ran into the service entrance directly across the street. Well, there was that family's Christmas dinner arriving!

Behind her, Arabel began to cough again. It sounded deep down inside her chest. Emmy turned to her sister quickly. "Arabel, you really must let me get a doctor for you. You're getting sicker and sicker!"

But Arabel shook her head stubbornly. "It's only a cold, Emmy. I've had much worse colds than this, *many* times. We don't know any doctors here, and they would be terribly dear and, well, right now we can't afford to waste money. Now, just let me rest, and I'll be fine by tomorrow." She turned over on her side and closed her eyes again.

Emmy stood looking down at her sister for a moment with a dull, worried, sinking feeling deep inside her. Arabel was very smart about some things, like becoming a teacher and wanting to come to New York and be a success and all—but about other things she didn't have very good judgment. Aunt Hannah knew it, too. That was why she had told Emmy to take care of Arabel.

The fire was dying down. Emmy went to the coal scuttle and shoveled several lumps into the stove. She was glad Mrs. Piddleby had left the key to the coalbin. She would pick it up when she went downstairs.

Right now, she would tidy up the room, and then she would go to Mr. Hoffelmeier's. When she was through with her work, she would come home and bring the kettle of soup Mrs. Hoffelmeier had sent word yesterday that

she would make because "soup was so good for a sore throat."

Arabel was stirring fitfully in an uneasy sleep as Emmy came back an hour later. Her forehead was very hot, and she moaned a little each time after she coughed.

"Oh, Arabel!" Emmy bent over her anxiously. "Don't you think I'd better get a doctor now?"

"No, no, no," said Arabel stubbornly, her voice no more than a whisper. "Just let me rest. All I need is *rest*."

"But don't you want some of the hot soup Mrs. Hoffelmeier made especially for you? It smells so good!"

Arabel turned her face away and closed her eyes again.

Emmy put the last of the coal in the stove and went downstairs with the scuttle to get more from the coalbin. She looked for the key on the downstairs hall table, but it wasn't there. Emmy went up and down the hall looking for it, thinking perhaps it had been knocked off the table accidentally. But there was no key!

Emmy went back down the hall and into Mrs. Piddleby's kitchen. There was a half-full scuttle of coal beside the kitchen stove. Emmy emptied it into hers and carried it back upstairs. Well, that was all the coal they would have for the two days. The key wasn't to be found, and the coalbin was securely locked. Emmy sat down in the little cane-bottomed rocker and began to think hard. She knew Arabel was really feeling worse all the time, no matter what she said. She knew, too, that now, of all times, she mustn't let the room get too cold.

Emmy got up and went to look in her reticule. She

counted the money carefully. Well, there. She had enough money to buy some coal from the coal man if she only knew where to find him. She took one last look at Arabel who was dozing, and tying on her bonnet, she picked up her cloak and went downstairs again.

How silent the house was—and dark! The day was so overcast that the depths of the hall were lost in shadows as if it were evening. Emmy sniffed. Even though the Piddlebys were gone, there still remained an odor of clams hanging in the air. Emmy supposed the house was saturated with the smell.

Hurrying down Broadway, Emmy had to push and thread her way through the crowds of shoppers. Christmas wreaths brightened the shop windows, and merchandise was displayed at a reduction for last-minute sales. Emmy paused just for a moment in front of the ribbon store. Oh, what a beautiful length of cherry-colored satin ribbon! Just the color that set off Arabel's dark hair and eyes. Emmy took a deep breath and went into the store. She just *had* to buy that ribbon for Arabel's gift. She had been waiting to do her shopping until today when she would have the full benefit of this last week's wages at Miss Serena's and Mr. Hoffelmeier's.

The length was too dear for Emmy to buy. She counted her money twice, but of course she must save enough for the coal man. She needed to buy bread and a cheese, too, and more tea and perhaps a roasted turkey leg at Mr. Hoffelmeier's for dinner tomorrow. She must try and make things cheery and Christmasy for Arabel.

"I'm afraid it's too dear," Emmy explained to the woman behind the counter. She looked longingly at the ribbon one last time. "It's *such* a pretty color!"

"Well, now, just a minute—if you like the color so much, here's the same color, same satin, only just half as wide, but very pretty, very pretty." She looked at the price marked on the ribbon. "And only half the price. How's that?"

Emmy would rather have had the very wide length, but this was the same pretty color and, after all, it was a good width for a lot of purposes. She looked up happily. "I'll take it."

On the corner, she bought a pennyworth of holly from an old lady selling it from a basket. "Merry Christmas, child!" said the old lady, and Emmy said, "Merry Christmas, ma'am," and felt nice and warm inside.

A few snowflakes began to fall. On the next corner a man was selling roasted chestnuts, and the smell was delicious! Emmy hurried by quickly because she didn't dare buy anything else with what remained of her money. She made her purchases at Mr. Hoffelmeier's, who insisted on putting in extra salad as "a little season's greeting" and then a jar of olives for "a Christmas feeling" and a fresh baked stollen and some Christmas cookies for "just a little gift." Emmy thanked him repeatedly, and they wished each other a Merry Christmas.

The snow was coming down heavily by the time Emmy reached Mrs. Piddleby's again. She came in and dusted the snow off her coat and bonnet before she closed the door.

Leaving the food on the kitchen table, she went up the stairs to Arabel, who was tossing restlessly and had thrown the covers off. Emmy quickly covered her again and emptied the remainder of the coal into the Franklin stove. There! Now she *had* to find that coal man!

Arabel moaned a little and turned over again. "Don't make such a noise," she whispered hoarsely. "Aunt Hannah, please don't rattle the stove lids. Aunt Hannah—"

"Aunt Hannah?" Emmy whirled and stared at her sister.

Arabel made a little gesture in the air with her hand and then let it fall heavily. "Aunt Hannah, I don't want any soup," she mumbled and rolled her head back and forth on the pillow. "No, no—"

Emmy suddenly was very, very scared. "Arabel! Arabel! It's me, Emmy. Don't you know me, Arabel?" She bent over her sister and smoothed her hair back from her forehead. She felt so hot!

"Aunt Hannah—Aunt Hannah—"

Emmy put her hand on Arabel's lips quickly. She couldn't bear to hear her say it again. Then she said, "Be very quiet, Arabel. Rest now and I'll be right back. You try to rest."

Emmy snatched up her cloak and bonnet with her reticule and ran down the stairs as fast as she could. In a daze, she leaned against the door for just a second before she opened it. "Oh, Arabel!" she whispered. If only Lissa and her grandfather and Captain Andy were not away in Long Island, spending the week end with their Uncle Bertie Spenlow! Even Trippey and Charlie had gone to

Trippey's sister's house for the Christmas holidays. She must get help quickly! Quickly! Miss Serena! She'd run down to Miss Serena, and surely she would know a doctor close by and could tell her how to find the coal man.

Emmy ran down the steps to the street brushing her hand across her eyes. It's the snow, she told herself, but she knew it wasn't true. The tears just wouldn't stop coming. She ran all the way to the corner and, as she rounded it, she collided with something very large that said, "Oof!" It was Mr. Bramble! And beside him was Aunt Abbie, looking gay and happy, and she was saying, "Emmy! What luck! We were just coming to call for a minute to leave these gifts— Why, Emmy! What is the matter, my dear?"

Emmy was never so glad to see anyone in her entire life! She just threw her arms around Aunt Abbie's neck and burst into a torrent of tears.

Mr. Bramble put his arm around Emmy, too, and said something comforting in his deep booming voice.

"It's Arabel!" she sobbed. "She's gotten so sick. She kept saying she was going to be better, and she just kept getting worse. Now, she doesn't seem to know me and keeps talking to Aunt Hannah who is back in Geneva!" Emmy wiped her eyes again.

"Merciful goodness, Thornwell!" Aunt Abbie took Emmy by the hand, and the three of them half ran down the block to Mrs. Piddleby's.

"It's like a tomb in here!" said Aunt Abbie when they came into the hall. "And what is that odd smell?"

"Clams!" said Emmy. "Come this way," and she led them upstairs to the attic floor.

"Wait here," said Emmy. She peeked in the door and saw that Arabel was half dozing again. Emmy motioned for Aunt Abbie.

"Arabel, my dear. Can you hear me?" She put her hand on Arabel's forehead. "She's so *feverish!* We must get Dr. Renfer immediately!" She went to the door and spoke to her husband. "Thornwell, Arabel is a very sick girl, I'm afraid. We must get Dr. Renfer here just as quickly as possible!"

Mr. Bramble spoke rapidly. Aunt Abbie nodded, "Oh, thank you, dear. I'll wait here."

In a half hour, Mr. Bramble returned with Dr. Renfer. They all waited outside while the doctor made his examination. Presently, he came to the bedroom door. "Miss Thatcher is quite a sick young woman," he said gravely.

Emmy gave a little sob, and Aunt Abbie put a comforting arm around her.

"She must be moved at once to a more comfortable lodging than this one," said Dr. Renfer. "It is too cold here, and I understand from Mr. Bramble that the owners have gone away for these two holidays. Miss Thatcher needs care. We shall be extremely lucky if we are in time to ward off pneumonia."

"But moving her, doctor!" said Aunt Abbie. "Isn't it dangerous?"

"It is, but not so dangerous as leaving her here."

Mr. Bramble spoke quickly to his wife.

"Yes, Thornwell! Exactly what I was going to suggest. Dr. Renfer, we wouldn't think of letting Miss Thatcher be taken anywhere but our home. We have plenty of room, and we are very fond of Miss Thatcher. And her sister," she added, patting Emmy's shoulder affectionately.

The closed carriage was fetched, Arabel was wrapped in innumerable blankets and quilts, and Mr. Bramble himself carried her gently down the long flights of stairs to the waiting carriage. Even Arabel's head and face were covered with a thick warm wool shawl, and Dr. Renfer would not allow it to be removed until she was safely in bed in Aunt Abbie's guest room.

Everything had happened so quickly, Emmy had not had time to catch her breath! Aunt Abbie had insisted that Emmy help her throw all of her and Arabel's belongings into the valises and bandboxes, and they were brought along on the carriage's return trip. So here they were, bag and baggage in Mr. and Mrs. Bramble's house with Arabel being made comfortable in the guest room and Emmy happily settled in a pretty little room next door to it.

Arabel was coughing again, and Dr. Renfer was still with her. When he came out of her room a few minutes later, he said to Emmy and Aunt Abbie, who were anxiously waiting, "I've given her something to make her sleep. She must have absolute quiet, and these medicines must be fetched from the apothecary's at once."

"Mrs. Fibbins, our housekeeper, will take turns with me sitting up with Arabel tonight," Aunt Abbie told the doctor. "You must come down now, Emmy, and have some dinner."

Emmy suddenly realized she was starved! Now that she thought of it, she had had nothing to eat since her breakfast tea and muffin, and a clock somewhere downstairs was now striking eight o'clock.

Seated with Aunt Abbie and Mr. Bramble in the cheerful big dining room, Emmy couldn't imagine having a happier Christmas Eve. After all the uncertainties and worries of the long dreary day, she knew that Arabel was taken care of at last, safe and warm and in the hands of a good doctor. Emmy put her fork down and sighed. She hadn't realized how much responsibility it had been until now when the responsibility was taken from her.

Outside the dining-room window, Emmy heard the voices of carolers coming up the street. They stopped in front of the house and sang "The Coventry Carol."

"Oh, Thornwell," said Aunt Abbie softly. "Do you hear? Isn't it lovely?"

Mr. Bramble reached his hand across the table, and Aunt Abbie put hers in it. Then they reached for Emmy's hands, and there they sat, the three of them, holding hands around the table until the carol was finished.

"Merry Christmas," they said together. Then Mr. Bramble got up, opened the window, and asked the carolers in for something warm to drink before going on.

·⊙· 11 ·⊙·

THE PRUITT PRIDE

O N THE Sunday after Christmas, Lissa, old Mr. Spenlow, and Andy returned from Uncle Bertie Spenlow's in Long Island. They were shocked to hear of Arabel's illness and hovered about wanting to be of some assistance.

"I thought she looked pale the day of the wedding, Abigail," said Mr. Spenlow.

"She looked beautiful," muttered Andy as he paced back and forth restlessly.

"Aye," said Mr. Spenlow with a twinkle, "but pale."

"She was coming down with it then. If I had only known!" said Aunt Abbie. "That cold church and—"

"Well, old Renfer will pull her through," said Mr. Spenlow. "How is she this morning?"

"Improving, Dr. Renfer said, but she is still so extremely weak. And her voice! She can barely speak above a whisper."

"What a Christmas!" said Lissa sympathetically. "I remember when I was five years old I had the measles, and it just didn't seem like Christmas *came* that year at all! By the time I felt well enough to enjoy the holidays, they were all over and done with." She frowned, remembering. "I've always thought that some day I am going to have two Christmases in a row and catch up with the one I lost."

Andy paused in his pacing for a moment and tousled Lissa's curls. "I expect you'll *do* that, too, Lissa, my girl," he told her with a smile. He turned to Aunt Abbie. "I don't suppose anyone can see her for some time?"

His aunt shook her head. "She must be kept very quiet. Even Emmy has only been allowed to wave to her from the door."

After Mr. Spenlow and Andy had gone, Lissa and Emmy settled down to play with Lissa's family of dolls. They were small china dolls ranging in size from about three to five inches. What Emmy loved most was the fact that there were so many of them! There were two grandmother dolls and two grandfathers, besides mother, father, nine children, aunts and uncles and cousins, and all the servants.

"You take care of the Popperlys, and I'll take care of the Skittersons," said Lissa.

Emmy giggled. "Where did you ever get such funny names for them?"

"Cousin Andy thought up the names when he gave me the dolls three years ago."

"Cousin Andy plays *dolls* with you?" asked Emmy in astonishment.

"Oh, no! But he always has good suggestions. And see what adorable things some of his crew have made for my dolls!" Lissa handed Emmy a tiny rattle made for one of the doll children. It was delicately carved, and through the open fretwork she could see the little ball that made the rattle.

"Imagine!" said Emmy in wonderment.

"It's carved out of bone, and the seamen call it scrimshaw work. See this little box? It opens and closes and is hinged with tiny pins."

Emmy sighed. What perfection! And there was a diminutive rolling pin for the Skittersons' cook and a set of three pie plates with fluted edges and a chess set for Grandfather Popperly and a thimble for Grandmother Popperly—so tiny you could hardly see it. Of course Grandmother Popperly had china fingers and couldn't wear it, but it was tied around her neck with a bit of blue thread and looked very cunning.

Lissa and Emmy dressed and re-dressed the doll families, had them celebrate Christmas Eve and Christmas, and now they were making their holiday calls.

"Oh, yes," Aunt Sapphira Skitterson was saying to Mrs. Popperly the younger, "the holidays have been delightful. And to think they are almost over and the children will be going back to school Monday."

"Well, my dear," said Mrs. Popperly the younger, in a confidential tone, "I, for one, shall be glad. The house is in a complete state of upheaval! *Nothing* is in its proper place. I spent fifteen minutes this morning looking for my curling irons, and *where* do you suppose they were?"

"*Where?*" said Aunt Sapphira Skitterson.

"*Where*, indeed! In the buttery! Tucked under two firkins of cottage cheese."

Lissa went off into a fit of giggles and almost dropped Aunt Sapphira Skitterson. "Emmy," she said when she caught her breath, "I'd rather play with you than anybody!"

"And *I'd* rather play with *you!*" Emmy assured her, and the two little girls sat there smiling at each other, holding Aunt Sapphira Skitterson and Mrs. Popperly the younger.

In the afternoon, Andy came back for a few minutes. He had brought some flowers from Hodge's greenhouse. "Do

you think your sister could have these in her room?" he asked Emmy.

He waited in the back parlor until Emmy came down from Arabel's room. "Mrs. Fibbins says Arabel is sleeping now, but she will see the flowers when she wakes up."

Andy nodded and took a few turns up and down the parlor, pausing for a long moment at the window. "Tell Aunt Abbie, Lissa, to let us know if Miss Thatcher takes any change for the worse—or if I—if we can do anything."

It snowed off and on for the next three days. Lissa spent every afternoon with Emmy, and they played endless games of checkers and lotto and took the doll families through the most exciting adventures and had their tea with Aunt Abbie in front of the fire. Outside, it snowed and the wind howled, but inside it was cozy and warm and happy. Arabel was getting better every day but still coughed and had to be kept quiet. Emmy just drifted along as if she were in a dream and pretended she didn't know that, as soon as Arabel was well again, they would have to move back to Mrs. Piddleby's. Mrs. Piddleby had been kind enough and said she would hold the room for them and had even offered to send "some nice fresh clams for the patient." Needless to say, the offer was declined with thanks.

On the afternoon of New Year's Eve, Arabel sent word by Mrs. Fibbins that she simply must speak to Emmy—and alone.

"Now, she mustn't tax herself," warned Aunt Abbie as Emmy prepared to go up to Arabel's room. "I know she wants to talk with you after all these days, but don't let her overdo it, my dear. Dr. Renfer doesn't want her to exert herself, she is still so weak, and it may start her coughing again."

"I'll make her be careful," promised Emmy.

"Oh, Arabel!" said Emmy a few minutes later. She ran across the room to where Arabel lay in the great four-poster bed and threw her arms around her sister. "I'm so glad you're feeling well enough to want to talk! But you mustn't overdo it. Aunt Abbie says you are to be very careful."

Arabel had deep circles under her eyes and looked much, much thinner. Emmy was glad Aunt Hannah wasn't there to see her at that moment. She wouldn't think Emmy had done a very good job of taking care of Arabel.

Arabel smiled weakly and said, "Oh, Emmy! Hasn't this been the most dreadful thing? How can I ever pay all this back? And Dr. Renfer! I certainly didn't count on anything like this happening when I told Aunt Hannah and Uncle Ben we would get along just fine in New York all by ourselves!" Tears filled Arabel's eyes.

"Oh, don't cry, Arabel!" Emmy was sure her sister shouldn't be crying.

"And Miss Fenwick! Dr. Renfer says I cannot go back to teaching until he gives his permission." She found her handkerchief and wiped her eyes. "And accepting all this from Mr. and Mrs. Bramble! It will take me the next ten years to repay it all."

"Oh, Arabel! Everything will be all right, you'll see! I'll save all I make at Mr. Hoffelmeier's and Miss Serena's and maybe I can get more work and we'll give it all to Dr. Renfer and then—"

Arabel shook her head hopelessly. "I shouldn't have borrowed that last money from Uncle Ben. I promised him I'd pay it back this very first year at Miss Fenwick's. I thought I could," she said, fresh tears coming to her eyes.

Emmy could see that the sooner she got Arabel's mind

off all their complications, the better. Her sister was in no condition to dwell on troubles.

"Aren't Captain Andy's flowers beautiful?" she said, going over to where they sat on the mahogany table on the other side of Arabel's bed. "He's been here every day asking about you," Emmy told her. "Sometimes twice a day. And he wants to see you when you're well enough."

"No!" said Arabel, trying to sit up.

"Please lie down, Arabel! But why? Why don't you want to see Captain Andy? He likes you!"

Arabel suddenly began to cry again. "*Likes* me! Feels sorry for me, you mean! And I won't have anyone feeling sorry for me! I can take care of myself and you, too, if I can ever get out of this bed and on my feet again!" And for a minute, Emmy thought Arabel was actually going to try to do it. But Arabel sank back on the pillows weakly and closed her eyes for a moment. "*Likes* me!" she muttered. "When he's always laughing at me. And when he's practically engaged to that Clarenda Jeffers—"

"Oh, Arabel, that isn't really so!" protested Emmy. "I *know* it isn't!"

Arabel wiped her eyes and blew her nose. "Well," she said with finality. "I don't know why I'm even discussing it. I mustn't think of anything but getting back to my teaching at Miss Fenwick's. If there is one thing I am determined to do, it is pay back Uncle Ben for all his help and kindness." She turned to Emmy earnestly. "Can't you understand, Emmy? It's an obligation that *must* be paid. And all this must be repaid, too." She waved her arms about her. "You cannot go through life accepting things without—" She faltered and paused a moment, then said in a whisper, "And I don't care how handsome and wonderful he is—" She put her handkerchief over her eyes and turned away from Emmy.

Emmy stood staring at Arabel with a tightness in her own throat. She guessed she had never loved Arabel more in all her life. And maybe Arabel *was* stubborn and had the Pruitt pride, but suddenly Emmy felt the Pruitt pride wasn't such a bad thing to have, after all. Arabel was going to go ahead and do what she felt was right, no matter how much it hurt. Emmy looked off out the window and sighed. If she could only do more to help Arabel!

There was a knock on the door and the sound of Aunt Abbie's voice outside. "Emmy? May I come in, my dear?"

"Oh, yes," said Emmy and ran to open the door.

"How is our patient?" Aunt Abbie frowned a little, seeing Arabel's tearful face.

Arabel tried to smile, but it convinced no one.

Aunt Abbie smoothed the covers around her and patted her pillow. "You just rest awhile," she said soothingly. "It takes a lot of energy to talk."

A week later, Arabel was propped up in bed, appearing more like her old self except for a transparent look to her fair skin and those delicate shadows under her eyes. She had perked up enough to tie a red ribbon in her hair to please Emmy, and she had on a dressing gown of deep red velvet that Aunt Abbie had insisted that she wear in case of drafts. The fire was burning brightly in the fireplace and offset the gloomy weather outside.

It was midafternoon, and Emmy and Lissa were home from school. They were standing beside Arabel's bed at the moment, entertaining themselves, and they hoped Arabel, with the Popperly and Skitterson families. They had made hollows and hills in the puffy bedclothes and had deposited various members of the doll families in them.

"Here," said Lissa. "This is Theodore Skitterson going into the carriage house."

Arabel chuckled and moved her foot under the comforters. "I don't fancy the carriage house resting on my toes," she told them.

Emmy had laid out little paths in a careful design up near Arabel's elbow. "Now, don't move," she warned. "You'll upset Mrs. Popperly's boxwood garden."

"Oh, let's see," said Lissa. "Why, we could pretend it's a maze. Here is Southey Skitterson come to take Polly Popperly for a walk in the garden. She's going to go this way and he's going to go that way, and then they won't be able to find each other."

"Why?" said Emmy.

"Why what?"

"Why do they want to get lost?"

Lissa tossed her head impatiently. "It's more fun that way, silly. It's like a game, don't you see? That's what mazes were for."

Arabel picked up Mrs. Popperly's cook. "Well, I think the cook should be in the kitchen preparing tea." She held the doll in her hand and thought an instant. "I think I'll let her make a clamcake."

"Oh, Arabel, no!" said Emmy in horror.

Arabel leaned back against the propped-up pillows and laughed as if she were enjoying it very much.

"How good it is to hear you laugh!" said Aunt Abbie cheerfully as she came in the door. "I told Andy you were feeling so well today that I thought it would be all right for you to have him for a visitor—*for a few minutes*, mind," she said to Andy who had come in behind her.

Arabel gave a little gasp of surprise, but before she could say anything, Andy strode quickly to the bed and held out his hand. "How are you feeling, Miss Thatcher? You gave us quite a turn, you know," he said, smiling down at her.

"I never meant to," said Arabel, looking confused. "It was so stupid of me—"

Andy flashed his teasing grin. "To catch a cold?"

"I mean—" floundered Arabel. "Being such a nuisance about it all—"

"Now, none of that!" said Aunt Abbie firmly. "Andy, you may chat a *little* while I go downstairs and see about tea. I'll be back."

Andy stood looking at Arabel who stared at the coverlet and said nothing at all for a moment.

Lissa and Emmy looked at each other and then at Andy and Arabel.

"Perhaps we'd better help Aunt Abbie with the tea things," said Lissa, nudging Emmy with her foot.

"Yes, let's," said Emmy. There, that would give them a chance to talk.

"No!" protested Arabel firmly. She took a deep breath and said without looking up, "It was very kind of you, Captain Spenlow, to send all the flowers. Each bouquet seemed lovelier than the last."

Andy made no reply.

"It—it still seems strange to me to see summer flowers in January," she went on.

There was another silence.

How awkward, thought Emmy. Somebody ought to say *something*, so she tried with, "Do you see what we've made here, Captain Andy? A whole town. The Skittersons live on this side, and the Popperlys live on that side."

Andy bent over and inspected the town. "Very clever," he complimented them. "And who is the lady in Miss Thatcher's hand?"

Arabel gave a start and put the doll down. "It's the cook," she laughed shakily. "I think she was just about to prepare tea."

"Here, Arabel," said Emmy, to keep the conversation going. "You take Polly Popperly while I get these children to bed for their nap. Lissa has Southey Skitterson."

"Oh, yes," said Arabel. "I believe they were going for a walk in the maze."

Lissa started to walk her doll over to meet Arabel's when Andy quietly reached over and took it out of her hand. "I'll take Southey Skitterson," he said.

Arabel glanced at Andy quickly, but he was looking at

the doll. He turned it to face the doll in Arabel's hand. "Would you do me the honor, Miss Popperly, of taking a turn with me in the garden?"

Arabel hesitated a moment with a smile playing around the corners of her mouth. "Thank you, Mr. Skitterson. I believe I'd like to."

Lissa and Emmy nudged each other and giggled with delight at their fooling.

"Do you mind if we walk down the garden path instead of the maze, Miss Popperly? I feel I have already been lost in a maze for some time now and I'd really prefer—"

"But of course, just as you like. What do you think of our lovely summer weather, Mr. Skitterson?"

Andy glanced out the window at the driving snowstorm and chuckled softly. "Delightful—although perhaps a little dry and warm for June."

"Yes, but aren't these early roses heavenly, Mr. Skitterson?"

"Very pretty. But what is that odd-looking bug—all red and green speckled, with horns and thorns and a bushy tail?"

"Oooh!" shuddered Arabel. "Where?"

"On that leaf. The one you're holding in your hand."

"Ooooh!" squealed Arabel with real feeling.

Emmy and Lissa collapsed against each other with laughter.

Andy turned his doll to face Arabel's. "Do you know you look very beautiful today, Miss Popperly?"

Arabel flushed a faint pink and kept her eyes on the

doll. "Have—have you seen our mutual friends the Cartwrights lately, Mr. Skitterson? I'm told little Bartholomew Cartwright has come down with the mumps."

"Please don't change the subject, Miss Popperly. And couldn't you call me Southey?" asked Andy plaintively.

Even Arabel giggled. "I—I really don't know you well enough, Mr. Skitterson."

"You haven't given yourself much of a chance, have you?" said Andy seriously.

Arabel looked up quickly and then down again.

"I wanted to see you very much today, Miss Popperly, because I'm leaving soon."

Arabel squeezed Miss Popperly tightly. "When—when are you leaving, Mr. Skitterson?"

Lissa frowned at Emmy. "Southey isn't going anywhere," she whispered. "He works in the bank right here in this hollow."

"In two weeks, Miss Popperly," replied Andy.

"I suppose you will be gone for quite a while," Arabel said softly. Then she added, "Mr. Skitterson."

"This time, it is going to seem like a long while to *me*," said Andy gravely.

"I hope you will have a successful voyage, Mr. Skitterson." Arabel's head was bent low so that Emmy thought Andy could probably see no more than her dark hair and the bit of red ribbon she had it tied with.

"I wish I could understand you better, Miss Popperly," said Andy with a sigh.

Arabel looked up then and said with a tightness in her voice, "I'm sorry, Mr. Skitterson."

He stood looking at her with a troubled, puzzled expression. They were still holding the dolls in their hands.

Lissa shook her head at Emmy. "Somehow, it doesn't seem like that came out just right," she murmured thoughtfully. "Next time, *we'd* better do it."

Andy put down the doll and turned away to the fireplace for a moment just as Aunt Abbie came in, followed by Fibbins and the tea tray.

·•· 12 ·•·

EMMY KEEPS A PROMISE

DEAR Aunt Hannah," wrote Emmy and then paused.
She looked around the beautiful little room with the
sprigged wallpaper and the bright rugs and the cozy fireplace. A log snapped and fell, sending up a little shower
of sparks. Emmy's valise and bandbox were on the floor,
almost packed. Emmy sighed heavily. Mrs. Piddleby's was
going to seem colder and more forlorn than ever after the
comforts of the Brambles' house.

It isn't just the comfort, though, Emmy told herself
honestly. It's Mr. and Mrs. Bramble and Lissa and Mr.
Spenlow and Captain Andy. They've all been so wonderful, and staying here since Christmas has seemed like being
a part of their family. She pulled herself up shortly. Here,
now. That was no way to be thinking! My goodness, she
and Arabel would see them in the future. At least, she
hoped they would. Aunt Hannah and Uncle Ben had been
so alarmed about Arabel's illness that they had written
and insisted that she and Emmy come home to Geneva at
once. They were going to manage somehow to send them
their train fare.

Emmy picked up her quill pen and continued. "We are just about ready to go back to Mrs. Piddleby's. Arabel is feeling quite all right again, although she is still a little thin. She will begin at Miss Fenwick's next Monday. Miss Fenwick said she couldn't pay Arabel for the weeks she missed, but at least she didn't engage anyone to take her place. Please don't worry about us. We are fine. In answer to your question about you-know-what, *yes*, there is someone very, very nice who likes her." Emmy paused a moment and studied the nub of her quill pen thoughtfully. Andy had called several times since that first visit. He had been gay and entertaining and had made Arabel laugh with his nonsense, but each time, when he left, Arabel had been quieter and more withdrawn than before. Emmy sighed and dipped her pen into the ink again. "But Arabel says she can't think of frivolous things when she has debts to pay. Please don't mention this, Aunt Hannah, because you know it won't do any good. You were right, Arabel does have the Pruitt pride. Please don't send train fare right now because Arabel is determined to try and get us through this winter if she can. After that, I've been thinking we may have to come back to Geneva for good. I would sort of like to stay here in New York, though, Aunt Hannah. It's so exciting, and we have made such good friends. Give my love to Uncle Ben, and to you, too, Aunt Hannah. Your loving niece, Emmy."

She had folded and sealed her letter with the dark-red sealing wax on the little desk in the corner when there was a rap on the door. It was Fibbins.

"Captain Spenlow is in the back parlor, Miss Emmy. He'd like to see you a moment."

"Oh, thank you, Fibbins." Emmy smoothed her hair and went flying down the stairs to see Andy.

"Hello, Emmy!" he greeted her warmly. "I came by to have a word with Aunt Abbie, but I see she and your sister have gone out."

"It has turned so suddenly mild," said Emmy, "Mrs. Bramble said the air would do Arabel good. They said they were driving down to the Battery. They asked me to go, too, but I had promised I'd wait for Lissa who is coming over."

Andy was pacing restlessly back and forth again. He went the length of the parlor and paused before the windows. "Emmy," he said, with his back to her. "Could I ask you something—rather personal?"

"Me?" said Emmy in surprise. "Of course."

"You know, I'm sailing shortly— And before I go—well, do you know why—that is, did I—" He paused and then shrugged helplessly. "I don't even know what to ask—much less the answer to it." He laughed a little as if at himself. Then he began again. "It's about your sister."

He came back to Emmy and sat down opposite her in the mulberry wing chair. "Your sister is a very beautiful girl, Emmy."

Emmy smiled up at him. Was this what he wanted to tell her? "I know," she said.

Andy frowned and shook his head a little. "Only, it isn't

just on the outside. Inside, she's beautiful, too. I knew it the first time I heard her sing."

Emmy nodded. She knew what Andy meant.

"But why is she so—" He hesitated again. "Emmy, I hate to ask you this. It seems prying in a way, and I don't mean it to be. But, is Arabel—I mean your sister—interested in someone else? Someone back in Geneva? Is that why she is so—so distant?"

"No," Emmy was happy to assure him. "There *was* someone—"

"Of course," groaned Andy.

"No, no. Arabel wouldn't have him. She said she didn't love him and anyway she had to make a success of her teaching and she had borrowed from Uncle Ben to finish her education and now she had to pay it back and show Uncle Ben and Aunt Hannah she was worth their care and investment and—" Emmy stopped, feeling suddenly that she had said too much.

Andy was leaning forward now with a light beginning to shine in his gray eyes. "And there's no one else?"

Emmy shook her head.

He sat back again with a sigh. "Then I ought to face the truth," he said humbly. "She just isn't interested in me."

Emmy hoped she wasn't being disloyal to Arabel, but here was Captain Andy sitting opposite her looking so wonderfully handsome and kind and quite sad because he thought Arabel didn't like him. "Captain Andy, I don't know so much about these things, but I do know that

167

Arabel cries every time we talk about you, only she thinks you are practically engaged to Miss Jeffers and, even if you weren't, she's only a country school teacher and—"

Andy threw back his head and gave a great whoop of laughter. Then he got up and swung Emmy in a big circle and gave her a resounding kiss on the cheek! "Emmy, if it weren't for your sister, I'd ask *you* to marry me! Quick! Do you think we can find them down at the Battery?"

Emmy was so taken by surprise, she didn't know what to say. "Why—why, I guess maybe we could."

"Get your cloak and bonnet. Charlie's outside with the carriage."

"But Lissa—" Emmy had no sooner said the words than the door bell jangled.

"We'll take her, too," said Andy.

Five minutes later, they were careening across Fourth Street. Andy leaned out the window and called, "Drive over to South Street, Charlie, so we can avoid the Broadway traffic, and *crack on more sail!*"

"Isn't this fun?" crowed Lissa. "I love to drive fast!"

But Emmy didn't answer. Her head was in a whirl! Everything was happening so *quickly*. Had she done the right thing by telling so much to Captain Andy? What would Arabel say when she found out?

They reached South Street and rattled toward the Battery, past the rows and rows of ships that lined the wharves. The hundreds of bowsprits hung over them, and the air was full of enticing, spicy smells. Somewhere sailors were singing a sea chanty, and raucous orders were being shouted from captain to crew. Everywhere there was life and bustle.

As they neared the Battery, Andy was the first to see Aunt Abbie's carriage drawn up and waiting. He leaped out and walked briskly down the graveled path that circled the water's edge. Emmy and Lissa hurried after him, their skirts and bonnet strings flying. They made almost a half circle before they saw Aunt Abbie and Arabel on the path ahead talking to two other ladies.

When they drew closer, Emmy said, "Oh, no!"

Aunt Abbie and Arabel were talking to Cousin Jennifer and Clarenda Jeffers!

"Andy!" Aunt Abbie greeted her nephew. "What a lovely surprise! It's such a mild day, I thought the air would be good for Arabel."

Arabel was looking confused, and Emmy had a sinking feeling everything was going to go wrong again. If only that Clarenda Jeffers weren't there! And she was saying, "Oh, Captain Andy! The very person I wanted to see! I have two tickets for the concert tomorrow night, and Jennifer can't go. Will you take me, like a dear man?" She smiled up into Andy's face as if he had already said yes.

Andy looked at Arabel with his old gay, teasing smile, and he said, "I'd love to, Miss Jeffers—but you see Miss Thatcher and I have an engagement tomorrow evening."

Arabel gasped.

Before she could say anything, Andy rushed on. "And if you will excuse us now, I have to whisk these ladies off."

169

He bowed to Miss Jeffers and Cousin Jennifer and, taking Aunt Abbie on one arm and Arabel on the other, he did, indeed, whisk them off down the graveled path so fast that they were out of breath when they reached the carriages.

"Here we are," said Andy when they reached Aunt Abbie's carriage. He opened the door, handed his aunt in, then, before they could protest, he lifted in first Lissa, then Emmy.

"But we came with *you!*" said Lissa, putting her head out the window.

"And *I* came with Mrs. Bramble," protested Arabel.

"You are going *back* with me," said Andy firmly.

Arabel was beginning to look apprehensive. "But I still

have so much to do," she explained hurriedly. "I haven't finished packing and—"

Andy grinned down at her. "Reef your sails, Miss Thatcher," he said. "It's the best thing to do in a gale."

"But—"

"Will you be back for tea?" Aunt Abbie called to them.

Andy shook his dark head. "I am taking Miss Thatcher to tea at Delmonico's. *Unchaperoned*," he added, opening his mouth to show Lissa and Emmy how they looked. Then he grinned and waved to them.

Arabel was still protesting, and Emmy and Lissa hung out the window so they wouldn't miss anything. Andy opened the carriage door, but Arabel stopped again.

"It is absolutely *necessary* that I pack, Captain Spenlow!" she insisted desperately.

"And it is absolutely *necessary* that I talk to you, Arabel," said Andy.

There must have been something in his voice that changed Arabel's mind, for she turned without another word and stepped into the waiting carriage. Andy got in after her and, leaning out the window, he called, "Cast off, Charlie!"

"Well, I never!" said Lissa and gave Emmy and Aunt Abbie a tremendous, excited hug. "Do you think—?"

Emmy felt limp. "*I* don't know. I wouldn't even guess!"

"Well, I think *I* know," said Aunt Abbie. "And I am so delighted I don't know what to do! I can't wait to tell Thornwell that Andy and Arabel are going to be engaged. He'll be so happy and so will Father."

"Engaged?" gasped Emmy. "Do you really think so?"

"Well, I know Andy," smiled Aunt Abbie. "And I'd say he looked very determined. Of course, I've known for some time how the wind was blowing."

Lissa and her aunt chattered happily all the way back to the Brambles' house on Lafayette Place, but Emmy sat in a daze wishing someone would pinch her. Was she dreaming or was all this really happening? She felt all mixed up inside, suddenly. She just loved Captain Andy and adored Arabel and this was exactly what she had wanted for them—but it had all happened so quickly! Emmy frowned and bit her lip. It was just that she had never thought beyond the point where Arabel found someone *just right*. Now, she and Arabel wouldn't be together any more, and Emmy would have to go back to Geneva to Aunt Hannah and Uncle Ben.

Mr. Bramble came home and, when he had heard the news, promptly dispatched Fibbins to ask old Mr. Spenlow to dinner. When they told Mr. Spenlow what they suspected about Andy and Arabel, he was so pleased that he just kept slapping his knee and saying, "By my topsail! I didn't think he was going to bring it off! By my topsail!"

Emmy looked around her happily, grateful to them because they were so fond of Arabel. Deep inside her, though, was that sinking feeling of loss. What a terrible person she was, she scolded herself mentally. To think of a thing like that at a time like this! Of course, she had always known Arabel would marry sometime and leave her! My goodness, wasn't that what she had been working on all this while?

It was almost the dinner hour when Andy and Arabel came in. One look at their faces told everybody what they wanted to know without their asking.

"Oh, Arabel! Andy! My *dears!*" said Aunt Abbie and burst into tears. Mr. Bramble had to put his arm around her and get out his handkerchief for her. He said something to Lissa. "Uncle Bramble says Aunt Abbie always does this when she's happy!" she told Emmy with a grin.

"You haven't heard the news yet!" protested Andy. "Arabel has promised to marry me!"

"Of course, my boy, of course," said old Mr. Spenlow. "We didn't mean to take the wind out of your sails, but you see the way you looked when you came in—and then we'd all been hoping—" He took Arabel in his arms and gave her a fond kiss on the cheek. "I can't tell you how delighted I am, my dear Arabel."

Emmy ran over to her sister then and held her tight and kissed her on both cheeks. "Oh, Arabel!" she said.

"How about me?" said Andy, bending down and holding out his arms. "You'll have to share those with me now."

Emmy gave him a big hug, and he kissed her on the tip of her nose.

Now Arabel was beginning to cry, too, and Andy had to put his arm around her and get out *his* handkerchief. He and Mr. Bramble exchanged knowing grins.

Emmy and Lissa were dancing around excitedly while everyone congratulated the young people.

They were still talking of it as they sat at dinner.

"And when is it to be, my boy?" said old Mr. Spenlow. "Do you want me to delay the sailing of the *Dauntless* until after the wedding?"

"When I return next summer," said Andy. "Arabel wouldn't agree to anything else."

"There are obligations I must repay," said Arabel simply. "And since I cannot manage them all by then, Andy has promised me I may teach next year, too—and as long as I wish."

Andy grinned. "I was ready to promise anything," he said.

Arabel looked radiant! Emmy guessed she had never seen her look so beautiful and so happy. With a pang,

Emmy realized she wouldn't see Arabel very often after she was married.

Emmy was so busy with her own thoughts that she was startled to hear Aunt Abbie saying, "But, Father, we want her here with us!"

"Nonsense!" said old Mr. Spenlow gruffly. "Isn't it bad enough that you have left us? Now you want to keep Emmy, too?"

"Emmy must live with *us!*" agreed Lissa emphatically. "But we'll both come over and spend the night with you often."

"Just a minute!" said Andy, holding up his hand for silence. "You're forgetting something, aren't you? Emmy belongs to *us*. We're going to find a house close by, and we can't move in without Emmy."

Lissa frowned. "Well, you can spend *half* the time with us, can't you, Emmy? And you can stop working for Mr. Hoffelmeier and Miss Serena and play with me instead."

"No," said Emmy. "I'm going to keep on working, too. I'm going to help Arabel with those obligations."

Emmy and Arabel exchanged a long, happy heart-full kind of look. Emmy grinned at herself then. She guessed that, after all, there must be some Pruitt in her, too.

Aunt Abbie was saying, "Well, you both are going to stay right here with us until the wedding, Arabel and Emmy. You cannot refuse us. We shall be too hurt! Besides, I love a wedding, and we have so many plans to make and—"

Suddenly, Emmy felt so bursting with happiness that

she knew she wouldn't dare speak. But she wished she could do something to express what she was feeling—

"Clams, Emmy?" said old Mr. Spenlow, passing a large platter of fresh raw clams.

Emmy stared at them a moment and then grinned a big wide grin. Why, even the clams looked good! She took two on her plate and ate them with horse-radish and hot pepper sauce—and they tasted delicious!